LIAR

FIONA COLE

To Serena
I couldn't keep it together without you.

PLAYLIST

Hotel Room - Calum Scott
Million Reasons - Lady Gaga
Lonely Together - Avicii (feat. Rita Ora
Close To Me - Ellie Goulding, Diplo, & Swae Lee
Bad Liar - Imagine Dragons
Chances - Backstreet Boys
I'm Not Calling You a Liar - Florence + The Machine
Girl With One Eye - Florence + Machine
Stronger - Ziggy Alberts
Hurt Somebody - Noah Kahan & Julia Michaels
All I Want - Kodaline
If Our Love Is Wrong - Calum Scott
Where It Stays - Charlotte OC
Someone You Loved - Lewis Capaldi
Counting Stars - OneReplublic
Liar - Camila Cabello
Mother - Charlie Puth
Shameless - Camila Cabello

The Scientist - Corinne Bailey Rae
Blackout - Freya Ridings
Legends - Now United
Peer Pressure - James Bay (feat. Julia Michaels)

1 OLIVIA

REMEMBER that time I fucked an older man in a sex club?

I think that was when I peaked in life. Can you peak at nineteen?

I rubbed my thumb across the creased paper pinned to my Kate Spade planner. I'd folded and refolded it so many times, taking it everywhere with me as a memento. My fingers stroked across the sharp lines of his initial like maybe I could get back the feeling of touching him just by feeling the dent of his forceful strokes. Anything to cling to the night, I felt alive.

Thank you for last night.

- K

"Please be sure to have your business selections to me next week," Dr. Arden said from the front of the room. I slapped my planner closed and shoved it in my leather tote, standing with the rest of the students who were hustling to leave class. "I know a few of you have been procrastinating on making a decision. If you don't come with a selection, one will be made for you from the list of local businesses."

I was one of those people, and as I walked past her desk, I knew—just knew—that if I looked up, she would be pointedly staring at me with disapproval. So, I kept my head down and got out of there. I needed to find something fast because that list of her options was lame, and I didn't want to spend the rest of the semester with a clock and jewelry owner. Not that I knew who I *did* want to intern for. Hence, why I'd been avoiding the assignment. We needed to find an unpaid internship for the semester and create a mock business based on what we'd learned.

I didn't intentionally put it off; I was just waiting for something to excite me—to make me excited like I'd been when I first chose my business major. I took a deep breath of the cold air and tried to remember that feeling. A feeling that faded with each passing semester. I dropped my head back and exhaled hard into the blue sky, trying to figure out what was missing. Why I'd been plagued with this boredom. Boredom that wasn't just in college. Boredom with life.

"Are you trying to see if the sky is falling?" my best friend, Oaklyn, said, walking up beside me.

"Nah, just hoping for a sign for my business project."

"You still haven't picked one?"

I stuck with the trend of the day and avoided her eyes too. At least, I tried. I peeked at her in my peripheral. She was currently swiping long wisps of her hair out of her face where the wind had blown it. It took the effect of her glare down a notch, but the sun making her light brown eyes shine gold like a little fire of accusation, boosted it back up.

I rolled my eyes at her glare and started walking.

"What about Voyeur? I'm sure Daniel would let you shadow him." She barely got the words out around her twitching lips.

"Oh, yeah. That would be great. I can see the PowerPoint

presentation now." I deepened my voice and said, "And on slide seven, you'll see that gang bang is the most requested performance among women."

Oaklyn laughed. "Actually, it's usually just a threesome."

I stopped walking and stared at her. "And you just look so innocent."

We laughed and started walking again.

"You know you could always go to your dad's business," she suggested falling in step beside me.

Another eye-roll. "Ugh. Gas and gas parts? No, thank you."

"You're such a diva."

I opened the door to the dining hall and blew her a kiss when she walked past. "You love me."

"Unfortunately," she grumbled with a smile.

"Whatever, you're lucky to have me. In fact, lunch is on me."

"Olivia..." she groaned.

She hated when I paid, but I did it anyway. I had enough money to pay for breakfast, lunch, and dinner for her entire college term, but her pride prevented it. Her pride also prevented her sexy-as-sin professor-boyfriend from paying either. At least he got her to move out of her shit box apartment and in with him.

"How's Callum?" I asked, changing the topic.

She put her wallet back in her bag with a sigh but took the bait. "Good. We're good."

"And the sex? How's that?"

"Olivia," she whisper-shouted.

"What? He's ridiculously hot, and I may still have fantasies from when we had him for class."

She glared and walked off to get in line, ignoring my laughter.

We had barely sat down when a deep voice spoke right behind me. "Hey, Livvie-baby." I clenched my jaw at the nickname and looked across the table to find Oaklyn, not even bothering to hide the look of disgust from her face.

"Hey, Aaron." I turned and smiled at him over my shoulder.

He sat his plate down and straddled the bench beside me. "You want to hang out tonight?"

'Hang out' was the equivalent of Netflix and chill. He wanted to know if I wanted to get together to fuck, and after thinking about my morning, sex sounded good.

"Sure." I pretended to ignore Oaklyn's scoff.

"Awesome. Let's do seven-thirty. The guys will be gone tonight, so no one will hear you."

He leaned in and placed a quick peck to my cheek, and I fought to not pull away. I didn't like PDA from Aaron. He wasn't my boyfriend—at least not anymore. He served his purpose, and it wasn't to paw me in public. Once upon a time, he'd been my main priority. I'd made sure I looked good for him. I'd made sure I was available for him. I'd made sure I bought the best lingerie for him.

Then he shattered the affection I'd poured into him, sucking my happiness right along with it. I'd been...depressed, and Olivia Witt did not do depression over boys. So, I'd picked myself back up, promised to never fall again, and used him for all he was worth. Of course, for my pleasure alone. I had control. I had a say of how it went and how it ended.

My phone buzzed on the table, and I swiped to find a message from my mom.

Mom: You should come by dinner tonight. Uncle Daniel is bringing a business associate, Alexander. He's an older gentleman who's been working in hotels for a while. He may be a great person to talk about your project to.

My mind conjured an image of an old man, clinging to his business to hold off retirement. His hotels were probably the

Holiday Inn, and that sounded about as appealing as the clock and jewelry owner.

I quickly texted her back, letting her know I had plans tonight. I could imagine her pinched lips and disappointment. I just didn't want to deal with my parents asking me about my plans—my future. I was a junior and had plenty of time to figure it out. Not that they cared beyond what they could brag about to their friends. I would miss Uncle Daniel though. I'd just have to make a point to schedule a lunch this week to make up for it.

"Shit," Aaron said, looking around his plate. "Forgot my silverware. Be right back, babe."

As soon as he left, Oaklyn leaned across the table and asked, "Why?"

"Why what?" I stuffed a bite of meatball in my mouth and played dumb.

"Why do you still hang out with him. He cheated on you. He doesn't deserve to breathe the same air as you, let alone have sex with you."

I stared down at my fork twirling noodles on the plate. Aaron had cheated on me. I'd had the pleasure of catching him with his head buried between some girl's thighs in the library. But that was almost two years ago, and I was an island now—unable to be hurt. Having Aaron as my fuck-toy removed any chance of some loser weaseling his way in.

"It's better to sleep with the devil you know rather than one you don't."

"Olivia..."

There was that warning tone in her voice. The one that said she was about to give me a monologue about how I was doing a disservice to myself by settling. I held up my hand before she could start. "I just turned down dinner with my mom, so I didn't have to hear it from her. I really don't want to hear from you either."

Her shoulders heaved up and down with her sigh. "I just worry about you."

"Why? I have everything I want. More than I need. What's there to worry about?"

"You shut yourself off from possibility. It's like each year you try less and less. I don't get it."

"I'm not shutting myself off. I'll tell you the same thing I tell them. I have my whole life to be busy—to work. Why pile everything on in college when I should be having fun? Why be so serious?"

"But you're not having fun. You're just sitting there waiting for something to happen to you, and you're wasting time by not trying."

"No, I'd be wasting my time if I tried, and it didn't work out. I want it to be worth the effort—to feel something for what I'm giving my time to."

"You give your time to Aaron and don't feel anything for him."

"That's a lie. I feel quite a lot when I'm with him. A lot of pleasure." She didn't find my humor funny when I waggled my brows. "Listen, I'm not just sitting here not doing anything. I know I'm not part of any clubs or signed up for any internships to test out the business, but it's not wrong to wait for something that you enjoy. I have a whole other year left of college to figure it out, and I'm bound to find something that sparks my interest. Until then, I have plenty of things that are fun. Design. Shopping. Hanging out with you."

She looked unconvinced, but I could tell she would let it go. "I just worry about you."

"And I love you for it."

Her eyes flicked behind me, and her whole body stiffened, shoulders coming back, and fists clenched like she was preparing for battle. I looked behind me to find Aaron brushing some redhead's hair back and leaning down to kiss her cheek. I took it in...and felt nothing. None of the hurt I'd felt when I caught him cheating. And that feeling of nothingness was why I was okay with settling for Aaron.

I knew what to expect and got what I needed from him.

However, I didn't appreciate his lips being on another just after they were on me. I didn't care that he was with other girls, but I did care that he would be so disrespectful to do it right in front of me.

"That motherfucker," Oaklyn growled.

I shifted back forward and forked another piece of meatball, taking a bite with a shrug.

She finally looked away from Aaron and shook her head at my lack of caring.

Aaron plopped back down next to me, vibrating the bench. "Hey, Livvie-baby. Can we push the time to eight-thirty? I forgot I had something to do."

More like some*one* to do.

My irritation spiked a little, and I couldn't imagine seeing him tonight. I was having a hard time seeing him right now without giving in to the cringe pulling at my face.

All of a sudden, the dinner with my family and the wrinkly, old Alexander sounded pretty appealing. I popped a bite of salad in my mouth and turned to him with a bored stare.

"Actually, I can't. Plans with the family. Sorry."

His face crumpled, and that, mixed with Oaklyn's snicker, had my spirits rising. Enough to give a genuine smile.

See, I had fun.

2 KENT

"Kent," Daniel greeted me at the door with a smile. He opened the door wider and gestured me in with a heavy pat on the back. "I'm glad you were able to make it."

"Yeah, my flight landed a little earlier than I thought." I still had my suitcase in the car.

"Hey, man," Daniel's brother, David, said. "Hope the flight wasn't too bad. I saw the snowstorms rolling into New York."

"Yeah, wasn't sure I was making it out today."

"Well, be lucky you did. Julia made my favorite: pot roast."

My mouth watered at just the thought of a home-cooked meal, which reminded me, I needed to visit my mom soon.

Julia was David's wife and had an affinity for cooking, even though she only saved it for her family and friends.

We all walked through the open foyer and into the dining room. The room was formal with a china hutch and chandelier but had a mix of paper napkins and tin containers on the table. The Witts' were an odd mix that blended perfectly. Daniel and David came from humble beginnings, while Julia came from a high-society house. Which led to the current situation on the dinner table, a perfect representation of them as a family.

"Hello, Alexander." Julia gave me a radiant smile. Just as bright as her blonde hair that was familiar and had memories, I struggled to repress, rising. She set the two bottles of wine on the table and came over to give me a hug and kiss on the cheek. "It's been too long since you've let me feed you."

Almost two years, to be exact. I'd hesitated looking them in the eye knowing what I'd done to their daughter. Hell, it had been hard enough to look Daniel in the eye, but I couldn't avoid my business partner and best friend.

"You boys always get together and leave me out," she mock-pouted but also gave me a wink.

"How dare we?" I said, hand to my chest. "Next time, I'll make sure we get reservations at the best restaurant in town for four, rather than the dingy bars us boys hang out in."

"Good. I'll be able to stop my husband from stumbling home drunk."

"I very well can't let my baby brother out-drink me," David muttered.

Daniel laughed, sitting down in his seat. "At least *try* to not let me out-drink you. You never quite succeed."

David flipped Daniel off, and Julia slapped his arm. "You're grown men. Stop acting like children," she chided, but still leaned in to kiss him. "Can I get you anything to drink, Alexander?"

"I'm good with the wine. Thank you."

Julia was the only person to still call me Alexander. Well, her and my mother. Everyone else called me by my last name, Kent. Which was how I introduced myself most of the time.

I grabbed a seat next to Daniel and noticed only four place settings. A weight that had taken up residence on my chest the moment Daniel had told me I was coming to dinner at his brother's house finally lifted. I took a deep breath and asked, "Just the four place settings tonight?" I had to be sure.

Julia sighed as she poured wine for everyone around the table. "Yes," she said irritably. "I asked Olivia to come, but she said she had plans with her boyfriend."

My jaw clenched, and I was only able to nod. Not that I cared that she had a boyfriend. She was what? Twenty, now? Almost twenty-one? Imagining her with someone—especially someone her own age—shouldn't bother me.

"You'll have to meet her another time," David said.

The weight that had just lifted landed back on my chest with a thud. They had no idea I'd met Olivia before. Intimately. Repeatedly in a night's span.

Thankfully, David began telling Daniel about his new product line, and I managed to stay focused on the conversation and ignore the family portrait above the buffet table across the room.

I didn't need to look at her picture to remember her. She'd visited my dreams more than I cared to admit. Most women came and went, and I had no doubt Olivia would have been the same if I hadn't been constantly faced with my mistake, each time I saw my best friend. At least, that's what I reasoned why I dreamt of her blonde hair in my fist as I fucked her from behind.

Thank God, I didn't have to be faced directly with the source. One small blessing for the night.

As if God was laughing at me for speaking too soon, the front door opened and slammed.

"Hey," an all too familiar voice called through the doorway. "Sorry, I'm late. Plans changed, and I figured I'd come home to see..." her voice faded off when she came into the room, her eyes landing directly on me. "Everyone," she barely finished with a whisper.

God, I forgot how blue her eyes were. I forgot how vibrant

she was with her blonde hair and youth. She looked so much younger standing there in her black leggings and oversized sweater that fell to her fingers. Almost like she could still be a high school student.

I had to look away when even that last thought didn't stop my dick from twitching under the table. Because no matter what she looked like standing there, my mind and body remembered how much of a woman she was.

"This hotel room is massive," Olivia said, awe tinging her voice as she stared around the room.

I stared at her back—so much bared skin, I didn't know where to start. My cock ached even though I had only come not even an hour before. All I could think about was rutting against her like an animal. And while I had plans to use her tonight in ways her nineteen-year-old body had probably never been used, I wanted to ease her into it—give her at least three more orgasms before I buried myself inside her again. To do that, I needed to come again—to ease the throbbing begging me to fuck her.

She turned to me—still standing by the door, my hands in my pockets—with a wide smile, her blue eyes sparkling under the chandelier. I didn't return the smile. Instead, I held her stare and prowled toward her. "On your knees."

"Wha-what?" she stuttered, her smile falling.

"I know what it feels like inside that tight cunt, now I want to know what it feels like in your throat." She swallowed, and it had the throbbing pounding harder, a primal beat thundering through me. "Now, get on your knees."

Her tongue slicked out, and I couldn't stop the moan as I watched her nibble her full lips as she sank to the floor.

I stood right in front of her, her large doe eyes staring up at me with heat and innocence. Holding her stare, I began undoing my pants, the clank of my buckle echoing in the tiled room. She didn't look away when she heard my zipper. She didn't look away when *she heard the rustle of my pants opening enough to free my length. She didn't even look away when I used the head of my cock to paint her full lips with my pre-cum oozing from the slit.*

With one hand around my shaft, the other dug into her hair, fisting it tight. I yanked her head back and held my dick at her lips. She opened on cue, but my cruel grip in her hair prevented her from moving to suck me into her mouth. I stretched out the anticipation as long as I could stand it. Finally, I began easing between her lips and slowly slid inside her mouth, not stopping even when I hit her gag reflex. "All the way to the back," I ordered, pushing into her throat.

"Olivia," Julia's happy voice broke me from my memory to find my hand clenched around the fork and knife with a white-knuckled grip. "I didn't think you were coming."

"Umm," her eyes kept flicking to me as she tried to form words to respond. "I thought dinner with family trumped what I had planned."

"Of course, it does." Julia stood to grab Olivia a plate and utensils and set them up next to her—right across from me.

Olivia sat slowly, barely taking her eyes off me like I had a gun pointed to her head, and if she moved too fast, I'd shoot her.

"Hey, pumpkin," David greeted her.

"Hey, Daddy."

Each greeting was like a punch to the gut. In the moment of that night, our age difference and the fact that she was my best friend's niece had seemed inconsequential. Hearing her be called pumpkin and her using the word daddy—not for me—had me feeling like an old man, preying on the innocence of the world.

"Olivia," Daniel said. "I hope you don't mind, I brought a friend for dinner?"

Her eyes finally jerked away from me, probably realizing Daniel's hesitant tone was due to her reaction since she saw me

12

upon walking in. "Of course, not," she said perkier than seemed natural.

"Where are my manners?" Julia admonished herself. "You two haven't even met yet. Olivia, this is Alexander. Alexander, this is Olivia, our baby girl."

Olivia's lips pinched a little. "Alexander?" she asked slowly.

I gave the most neutral smile I could conjure and gave a slight nod. "Alexander Kent."

3 OLIVIA

Holy. Freaking. Shit.

Ohmysweetmothermaryjosephgodalmightyfuck.

Those were the only words rolling through my head, and I had to clamp my jaw shut to keep them from tumbling out. What did I say? Acknowledge we'd met? No, that wouldn't work because then they'd want to know where. What did *he* want me to say? Did he want me to pretend we'd never met?

When my mom nudged me under the table, I realized I'd been silent for too long and went with the easiest response I could muster.

"It's nice to meet you, *Alexander*." I couldn't stop myself if I wanted to from enunciating his name.

He'd told me his name was Kent. He'd told me a lot of things that night.

Suck my cock.

Swallow my cum.

Bend over.

Take more.

Scream for me.

But not once did he say his name was Alexander.

"Please," he said, his deep voice rippling over my skin. "Call me, Kent."

I could barely meet his dark eyes without my body trembling with remembered pleasure. But somehow, I managed to hold them, I managed to remain calm under them, despite the intense heat. I swallowed, becoming lost in memories of staring up at him as he moved inside me. The moment stretched and tightened, and I was sure it screamed at everyone in the room.

"Oh." *Way to sound eloquent, Olivia.* "Uncle Daniel, you never mentioned him." How the hell had I missed this connection.

"Sure, I did. He's the business partner I always talk about— maybe I never actually said his name. Kent owns the other half of Voyeur. Your mom usually shuts down all conversation before I can get very far."

A manic laugh bubbled up my throat, but I choked it down. "Huh." More eloquence spewing from my lips.

"That's enough of that talk," Mom stepped in as usual. She tried to shield me from Daniel's illicit club as much as possible. It was a hollow effort at best since I already knew everything there was to know.

"I started calling him Kent in college, and it stuck," Daniel said.

I blinked a few times, coming out of my stupor.

"I was sure it was because you just forgot my first name, and I was too lazy to correct you," Kent joked.

Daniel gave him a doubtful look and shook his head. "I was the best thing that happened to you in college."

"I remember you in college," Mom said with her eyebrows raised. "I'm not sure how good you were for anyone with your wild ways."

Daniel shrugged unapologetically and turned to me with the

sincerity I always saw from him. Sometimes my parents got caught up in their lives, friends, and appearances, leaving our relationship nice but superficial. Daniel, however, had always been there. He'd guided me through the hardest parts of life, answered all the questions no matter how uncomfortable they were. He saw the real me, and that was a rare occurrence the older I got. "Speaking of crazy college students, are you keeping out of trouble?"

I fought to keep my eyes from flicking to Kent's. "Of course, I'm an angel."

Dad snorted, and Mom laughed. Then I did look at Kent, who had an eyebrow raised, and gave me a look that said he knew better. Everyone else was making a joke, knowing I kept my life pretty uninteresting. But Kent...Kent knew I was anything but an angel.

I copied Daniel's movement and shrugged. "I keep good grades."

"Speaking of good grades," my mom said. I fought my eyes rolling back in my head. Here came the interrogation and suggestions for more. "Did you get the email I sent about the Honor Society. You'd be a shoo-in."

My eyes met Daniel's across the table, and I almost laughed at his eye-roll.

I kept my answer short without giving any ammo to continue the conversation. "Yeah, I saw it."

"And...?"

"And, I'll look it over." No promises or guarantees, that way, she couldn't hold it against me when I didn't join. Nothing about what the Honor Society did enticed me. I didn't care to go to the formals and stuffy meetings. If I wanted to do charity work, I didn't need to do it with a bunch of people I didn't even like.

"Would anyone like more to drink?" Mom asked. "Kent?"

"No, Julia. I'm good, thank you. Actually, I'm going to run to the restroom."

"You remember where they are?" Daniel asked.

Kent nodded and disappeared around the corner.

"He's been here before?" I asked, surprised I'd never met him in our home.

"Yeah, Kent and I go way back. He's been here quite a few times. I guess you've always just missed him."

And yet, I hadn't missed him that night at Voyeur. Interesting how things played out.

I looked over at the empty seat and quickly cleared my plate of the last bite. "I'm going to run to my room real quick. I need to grab some books for class."

I walked out and passed the stairs leading to my room and headed toward the bathroom in the hall. I needed to just say hi to him in private. I needed to look in his eyes without pretending we'd never met. I may not ever see him again after tonight. I mean, I'd somehow missed him for twenty years, what's to say I wouldn't miss him for another twenty.

I carefully twisted the knob, closing my eyes and sending a quick wish that it wasn't locked. When it fully turned, I bit my lip to hold back the smile trying to break free. I pushed the door open quickly and stepped in, shutting it softly behind me.

Kent's eyes widened over his shoulder as he rinsed his hands at the sink.

Leaning my back against the door, I stared for a moment, taking in his lean body, his dark hair sprinkled with bits of gray. I noticed his beard was trimmed and sporting more gray than it had when I'd last seen him. If anything, it made him sexier.

"Hi," I whispered. My intentions were innocent when I stepped through the door, but if he were to ask, I'd do whatever he wanted; right here with my parents only a room over.

His brows furrowed, and he swallowed hard, snatching the

towel off the rack and drying his hands with jerky movements. "What are you doing in here?" he whispered harshly.

I almost wanted to laugh at his nervous glances to the door like he expected someone else to barge in on us at any moment. "I was just saying hi, *Kent*."

He took a deep breath and sighed; his shoulders finally relaxing as he dragged a hand through his hair. "You shouldn't be in here, Olivia."

"I know. I just wanted to say hi without pretending we don't know each other." I gave a small smile. "I promise to not force myself on you."

He breathed a laugh. "Trust me, you wouldn't have to force anything." He fully faced me with all his attention. His features relaxed, and it reminded me of when we talked over snacks at midnight between fuck-sessions. He looked like the Kent I knew and not the frantic Alexander from ten minutes ago. One side of his lips tipped up, and he looked at me like a fond memory. One that wouldn't be repeated.

A sinking weight dropped from my chest to my stomach. I wasn't surprised by it—just surprised by how sad I was over the disappointment. I dropped my head to hide the deep breath I was taking to push past the weight tugging in my chest.

His shoes came into view, almost kissing the tips of mine. Then his hand appeared as it reached under to tip my chin. The heat from the singular, simple graze of his finger to my skin bloomed out from the spot, swelling my lips, making my nipples hard, and dipping down into my stomach, somehow mixing with the disappointment, fighting for dominance.

"You know I don't regret anything about that night, but if Daniel found out, it wouldn't go over well."

He was only voicing what I'd seen in his eyes a moment before. The disappointment won, and I didn't fight it this time. I cocked a brow and gave him my sexiest smirk, enjoying his fingers on my skin a bit longer before pulling back.

"I don't regret anything either. You know, in the moment, nothing seemed very important besides feeling you." I laughed softly, finally breaking the connection when I dropped my head back to the door. "But sitting with Mom and Dad at dinner with you was a strange situation, I wasn't expecting to face." He laughed with me, running his hand through his hair again. "Don't worry though. I don't plan on going out there and announcing that I know what it feels like to choke on your cock."

His eyes flicked to mine, heat making the dark brown look almost black. A growl rumbled low in his chest. I squeezed my thighs at the predatory look, my smile growing at how I could still affect this man. I couldn't help it. He stood there, so tall and broad—so mature. I knew how playful he could be, and I wanted to bring it out of him, just for me, in this tiny space.

"That's a good call," he managed to squeeze out past his clenched jaw.

I stepped away from the door and into him, fighting down the urge to push up to my toes and kiss his cheek. I wanted to smell his skin to see if it still smelled of the orange sandalwood that enticed me almost two years ago. But somehow, I did fight the craving and turned in the small space, my shoulder brushing his chest, and opened the door. I scanned the hall and before I stepped out, looked over my shoulder and gave a wink. "See you out there, Kent."

I quickly ran to my room and picked some random book to shove into my bag before returning to the dinner table. Kent gave me a cursory glance and seemed to have relaxed since our little bathroom chat. Probably feeling relief that I hadn't fallen at his feet and begged him for a repeat.

I grabbed a seat next to Mom, and she slid me a glass of wine.

My dad gave her an irritated look, but she waved him off. "She'll be twenty-one in a month. Don't give me that look, David."

I took a sip of the crisp liquid, the taste of apples, lingering in my mouth long after I swallowed the dry wine. I smiled around the rim of my glass when I noticed a muscle tick in Kent's jaw at the mention of my age.

"Olivia, how's your project going? Have you found a business to intern for yet?" my mom asked.

"Well, you won't let me work with Uncle Daniel, so I'm at a loss."

Daniel laughed and winked at me. "Nice try. We don't want to give your teacher a heart attack with your presentation. Or spoil that angelic mind."

According to my family, I only knew what Voyeur was from a few comments made here and there by Daniel and Dad. No one but Kent knew I'd snuck in and already corrupted my *angelic* side.

"Why don't you intern for Kent?" Daniel suggested. "I'm sure he can conjure up a spot for you."

All the relaxation that Kent had gained since coming back into the room vanished. His shoulders tensed, and his head jerked to Daniel.

"Ummm..." I hesitated.

Daniel didn't notice and kept talking up the idea. "Yeah, it'd be great. He's opening a new hotel here in Cincinnati, a big, ritzy one. It's in the end stages, so you'd get to see how the final business is set up. It'll be great."

"Um," Kent began. "I'm not sure that will work. I've got the one in New York too that needs me, and I won't be here very often."

"Nonsense," my mom said, waving her hand like she was swatting the problem away. "I've seen the project criteria. She only needs a few hours a week."

"And she could work with one of your managers if you happen to not be there," Daniel added.

They just kept talking, building up the plans, each idea making it harder and harder to turn down. Kent kept opening his mouth to speak, but they'd talk over him, shutting down anything he was going to say. I could tell he wasn't too keen on the idea but didn't have a leg to stand on to deny it.

"It's really up to Olivia if she's interested or not," he said when he finally had room to speak. His eyes gave a hesitant look. He probably wanted me to say no, to give him an out.

But for the first time since I'd agreed to fuck an older man in a sex club, my heart raced. My skin prickled with excitement like I had my hand on a battery, and the electricity worked its way through me. Oaklyn said I couldn't just sit by and wait for things to happen. She told me I had to take charge.

So, I ignored Kent's look and took charge.

"I'd love to."

4 KENT

"How long until you leave again?" Daniel asked from his lounged position in the club chair.

"In maybe a week or two."

"Always gone. You should at least buy an apartment here to give you a home-base."

I stared at the glass of amber liquid hanging precariously from my fingertips, entranced by the round ball of ice circling the bottom.

"My parents live here, and that's enough of a home-base for me." I lifted the glass and sipped the spicy drink.

Daniel smirked. "Can't exactly bring girls home to the parents' house."

I gave him my own smirk in return. "That's what hotels are for. And I just so happen to own one. Two pretty soon."

"You could always buy a place in my building. Olivia lives there too, so you can just join the brood, and we can slowly take over the entire building."

Olivia. That name had haunted me for the past week. More, if I had to be honest. She'd been haunting me for over a year. At least then, she was just an elusive memory. Now, she was a tangible, in my face, temptation. One I had to ignore, specifically because of the man sitting across from me awaiting a response.

"Why pay rent if I'm not going to be here half the year?"

"Like you can't afford it."

I shrugged and drained my glass, setting it on the wooden side-table. I was happy with my situation. I could leave my meager belongings with my parents and stay there when I needed. If I had company, I always took them to the hotel. Nothing personal, just a fun romp for a day or two and an easy out. Just the way I liked it.

I'd done the whole house and serious relationship thing a long time ago. I was better off without it. I was happier without it.

"Hey, boys," a husky voice greeted behind me.

Daniel smiled, and I knew I'd find a knockout brunette when I turned.

I wasn't disappointed. Carina's full lips were tipped in a barely-there smile, and an eyebrow cocked liked she'd find us *boys* up to no good. Mostly, she wouldn't be wrong, but tonight we were just two men enjoying drinks at our club.

"Hey, Carina." Daniel stood to give her a hug and gestured to the seat between us. "Did you have any trouble getting into the front?"

"Nope. Andre, let me in just fine. I come so often, I should just get a membership discount," she said, winking at Daniel.

She leaned over to pull papers out of her briefcase. I tried to be a gentleman and not stare at the curve of her breast exposed by her low-cut shirt, but I couldn't help myself. And when she leaned back up, she caught me staring and slapped the top of my head with her thick stack of paperwork.

"Ow."

"Don't be a pig."

"Don't be so gorgeous."

She rolled her eyes and began setting up her computer. Men all around us stared. Her long brown hair swaying over her shoulders, made a man want to wrap it around his fist. But when I imagined it, the color of hair sliding through my fingers was blonde. When I jerked her head back and made her stare up at me, her eyes were a paler blue, her skin like porcelain rather than Carina's tan.

"I don't know why we couldn't have met at the office," Daniel said.

"Voyeur always makes everything more interesting. Why not include our business meetings?"

Carina opened files, pulling up numbers that her counterpart, Jake, had run for the probability of success for each marketing plan. She was efficient without judgment of our business, therefore making her the prime candidate to handle our future projects.

"We're thinking of opening a club in New York."

Her eyebrows rose high at the news. "Leaving Cincinnati?"

"No," Daniel explained. "Just expanding."

"I'm in the process of closing on a location for the next hotel," I explained. "And we figured it was a perfect time and place to expand."

"And we were wondering if you'd be willing to take on the business. Only you," Daniel specified. Carina's father, the owner of their marketing company, doubted Carina's ability as a woman in the business field and tried to take the larger jobs for others. But we wanted to make sure she was the one handling us.

"Wow. Of course. I'd be honored to." Her eyebrows lowered and lips pursed. "I'm in the middle of another large project, but I should be able to make the occasional trip out and do everything else from here."

"Is Daddy letting you have another big project?"

She rolled her eyes. "Hardly. This one is more...freelance."

"Interesting."

"Can I get you anything to drink?" one of the waiters asked Carina.

"Just a water, please."

"Olivia starts with you tomorrow, correct?" Daniel asked.

Less than twenty-four hours until I was around the girl who visited my dreams more than I'd like to admit.

"Yeah."

"Why'd you hesitate?" Daniel asked.

I rubbed my thumb along my brow and thought of the best way to answer. Maybe try and find a valid reason out of this predicament. "I'm just worried she won't get what she needs. We aren't an up and running business yet, and I won't be around as much."

Daniel waved away my concerns. "She just needs to get a behind the scenes look, and what's better than how one is set up. And just pass her off on Viv. She is your manager."

"Who's Olivia?" Carina asked.

"My niece. She's a business major in her junior year and needs to shadow a business for a project."

Carina snorted. "And you don't think Kent will corrupt her? Lure her into where the real business is here at Voyeur."

I almost choked on my own tongue.

"Yeah, right," Daniel laughed. "Besides, she already knows about Voyeur. At least some of it."

I busied myself with drinking the new glass of bourbon, not pulling my lips away from the edge just to keep my mouth busy and out of this conversation.

"And you're not worried the notorious flirt won't hit on such young prey," Carina taunted. They were picking on me, making it a joke. But it felt like they were looking at my memories and pushing me to reveal it all.

"Ha!" Daniel barked a laugh. "While Kent is a womanizer, he's always kept it above drinking age."

God, help me.

As though my prayer was heard, a tall red-head came to stand beside my chair, her perfectly manicured nails scratching down my suit.

"Hey, Kent."

My eyes scanned her body as I moved them up to meet hers. "Hey, Sara. Good to see you."

She leaned down, giving me a more than generous look at her braless breasts and whispered in my ear. "I was hoping you could see more of me. Maybe in a private room?"

I wasn't one to look a gift horse in the mouth and latched on to my opportunity to escape with both hands.

"Absolutely," I said before capturing her plush bottom lip between my teeth. "Go make a selection and meet me in the back hall."

She kissed the corner of my mouth and walked away.

"See," Daniel said, gesturing with his glass to Sara's retreating form. "He likes his women mature enough to handle him. Olivia wouldn't be on his radar."

On that note, I drained my second glass and stood to go. "Carina, as always, a pleasure to see you. Call me, and we can set up another meeting." I turned to walk away but stopped and looked over my shoulder. "Enjoy a show on me tonight."

Her smile was slow and devious. She'd had a rough year, and I was happy to give her anything to clear the shadows from her eyes.

Before I reached the end of the hall, where I could see a flame of red hair waiting for me, I dived into the supply room and scanned the shelves for a toy. I looked at the various dildos and vibrators with less interest than I'd usually feel. I closed my eyes and imagined heading into the room and feeling Sara's soft body over mine, her warmth swallowing my length, the look of my handprint blooming along her skin. But none of it came.

Instead, Olivia's sweet, but devious smile and innocent eyes, were all I could see staring down at me as I remembered the flavor of her cunt on my tongue.

"Fuck," I grunted.

With a renewed focus to fuck Sara, I grabbed a large rotating vibrator and headed to my prize.

Once we entered the room, she kissed down my neck, stripped me of my jacket, and groped for my cock. I dug my fingers in her hair and pressed her to the floor, leaning her back against the glass, separating us from the scene beyond.

I barely noticed the woman performing on the other side of the glass, bent over the bed as the man whipped her with the belt, between fingering her ass. Standing to my full height, I imagined doing the same to Sara and faltered. All I saw was blonde. Fucking blonde.

I tossed the toy to Sara. "Spread your legs and fuck yourself with this. Let me see it all and don't come until I say to."

Sara and I had met at Voyeur a few years ago and occasionally met up if the time worked. She was used to what I wanted, so it was easy with her. She knew how cruel I could be and loved every second of it.

Which made me not touching her perfect. She wouldn't ask why I denied her my touch. She'd assume it was part of our game when, in reality, it was because I didn't want to disrespect her by fucking her as I closed my eyes and imagined another.

She pulled her panties aside and slid the toy up and down her slit before pushing it all the way in.

I sat back in the chair and watched, occasionally stroking my cock through my pants, but never pulling it out. I made her play with herself until she was sweating, flushed, and writhing on the floor. I made her hold her orgasm off for the full forty-five minutes in the room. Made her listen to the couple's moans as they got off. And then finally, I let her come. I relished in the cries she made, relished in the power that even without touching her, I made her come so hard.

When she was done, I stood and squatted down to her.

"Good girl." I placed a soft kiss to her lips and pulled the dildo slowly from her body. Standing, I held a hand out to her and helped her readjust her clothes but had no intentions of staying. I pressed one more kiss to her forehead and walked out.

I went straight home and stripped my clothes. The hot water of the shower welcomed me—embraced me—as I gave in and stroked my cock to images of bending Olivia over a bed and whipping her with my belt, imagining her cries to stop and for more. I imagined her heat and moaned out my release, coating the shower walls with my cum, turning the water to scalding to wash away the evidence of what I'd done.

So I could go back to pretending it never happened.

5 OLIVIA

"You WANT to grab pizza for lunch?" Oaklyn asked me from the edge of my bed.

"Can't." I swiped my lips with a bold red. "I have my first day of interning."

She perked up at that. "You finally found someone?"

"Yup. I ended up meeting Alexander at dinner, and I'm working with him."

"Is he as old and boring as you imagined?" she asked, laughing.

I smiled, remembering my words describing who I thought *Alexander* would be. "Umm..." I paused, trying to figure out how to explain. But then I remembered it was my best friend behind me, who was currently living with our older professor. Hell, she'd probably fucked on his desk just yesterday. I didn't need to filter my words. "No. He was actually the guy I slept with at Voyeur."

She sat upright at that, her eyebrows trying to become one with her hairline. "Excuse me?"

"Yeah." I turned to her and leaned my butt against the dresser. "Kent. Who is apparently really, Alexander Kent. My uncle's best friend. Also, the other half investor in Voyeur. And a hotel entrepreneur."

"That's a lot for one man."

I held up a finger. "Can't forget the best sex I've ever had."

"And he was at your parent's house?" I could hear the laughter she fought to hold back.

"Trust me, it was more awkward than you're imagining."

"Next time, message me immediately, so I can enjoy the show." She looked me up and down. "So, are you having sex with him again?"

Taking a deep breath, I pushed down the remaining disappointment that I couldn't quite kick. "No. It was a one-time thing that was easy to do without all the complications staring us in the face."

"You seem awfully excited about seeing him."

I smirked, giving a careless shrug. "It's the hotel, I swear."

She gave me a deadpanned stare. "And are you wearing the extra tight skirt and red lipstick for the hotel too?"

"Got to make a good impression on my first day." I turned around and stared at the blue eyes shining back in the mirror. They were wild and excited for the first time in years. But my eyes were easily drawn to my full red lips. Perfect. Exactly where I wanted the attention.

"Well, be careful. You wouldn't want Daniel to find out."

Looking over my shoulder, I reassured, "He won't. Because it won't happen again."

My flats didn't make a sound as I made my way from the carousel door to the man standing at the front desk.

He was hunched over with a woman next to him. One hand was resting on the table, his flexing forearms visible from where his dress shirt was rolled up. The other hand held a coffee, and I almost willed him to move it to his mouth, so I could watch his lips curl around the edge. Just the thought had me squirming.

The woman next to him, stood upright and noticed me first, giving me a bright smile. I almost faltered at how gorgeous she was. She screamed successful in her wide-leg slacks and cream silk blouse, and I couldn't tell if I was jealous of her confidence or the way she seemed so familiar with Kent. Was she his girlfriend? Was he screwing her? Had he screwed her like he had me?

"You must be Olivia," the tall brunette greeted me. "I'm Carina, the project manager. It's nice to meet you."

I saw Kent stand upright out of my peripheral, but I kept my attention focused on Carina. Kent didn't want a repeat, and I wasn't going to make a fool of myself by giving him every ounce of my attention. "Nice to meet you, Carina."

She collected the papers spread out on the table, filled with colors and drawings. "I'll get these organized and the final products ordered by the end of the week." And then she turned and left me with nothing else to do but finally face Kent.

I gave him a bland smile—one I would have given to a stranger on the street. "Good morning, Mr. Kent."

His mouth twitched as though he was fighting a smile, and as expected, his eyes dropped to my painted red lips. "Good morning, Olivia. And call me Kent."

"So, what's the plan for today?"

He stared for a long moment, his eyes assessing like if he looked long enough, he'd find an answer to a question I didn't even know about. If I did know, I'd help him answer it. Anything to lower the intensity of his gaze.

I kept my face neutral, but I couldn't stop the way my heart raced as the seconds ticked by. I couldn't stop the way I breathed harder to get more oxygen to my lungs, bordering on panting.

Finally, he looked away and took another drink of his coffee.

"I looked over the project outline you emailed last night, and I'm sure we can cross all these off before the deadline. We're in the final stages of completion. It will be the perfect time for you to observe." He moved to the back wall where a Keurig sat. "How do you like your coffee?"

He didn't ask if I wanted coffee. Apparently, his dominance extended further than the bedroom. "Black, please."

He froze and looked at me over his shoulder with an eyebrow raised. "I took you for a cream and sugar girl."

"Black like my soul."

He laughed and turned back to his task. Once the lid was firmly in place, he handed me my cup. I wanted to sigh when my fingers grazed his. The small touch was intimate and a reminder of how we were pretending we hadn't touched before.

"I'll take you around to meet everyone." He stretched his arm out toward the back and fell in step beside me when I began walking. "I have a meeting, but Vivian is the hotel manager and will be able to help you with any questions."

Thankfully, he wasn't looking and couldn't see the frown I couldn't stop. I was disappointed in myself for letting him simply not being there with me make me pout like a child. I didn't get emotionally attached. There was no need. I was twenty and had plenty of time. I wasn't in a rush to experience what Aaron had put me through two years ago.

Maybe I needed to take Aaron up on his offer and meet him tonight. I didn't have to stay. I didn't even need to have sex. Just go over, have him go down on me, and then get out. That idea had my frown turning upside down by the time we reached the rest of the workers.

Kent didn't waste much time doing the introductions before leaving like the building was on fire. Vivian took over just as promised. She looked just as professional as Carina, but twice her age and half her height. The confidence was the same, and I admired her for it.

I didn't expect much when I'd signed up for this, but I quickly found myself enjoying the topics. I asked more questions and actually made a suggestion to Vivian in one of their pow-wows. Her praise of my idea had me standing a little straighter. It had me eager for the months to come, and eagerness hadn't been part of my emotional repertoire in longer than I could remember.

It was the end of the day, and I was standing at the front desk with my elbow resting on the table and my chin on my hand. I was so focused on scrolling through the finance setup that I didn't even notice someone was behind me until a throat cleared roughly.

I checked over my shoulder to find Kent trying to keep his eyes from staring at my ass, perfectly displayed in the tight red pencil skirt.

"Like what you see?" I taunted.

He didn't respond, but his mouth tipped on one side, and that was enough for me.

"How was today?" he asked.

"Good. Your hotel is more entertaining than I was expecting."

"I aim to please."

"I remember."

Kent's jaw ticked. He took a deep breath, but again, didn't acknowledge my comment. "What are you looking at?"

"Financial setups. Vivian had me looking at the projected numbers from Carina."

"Let me check it out."

I expected him to wait for me to get out of the way, but instead, he stepped behind me and reached for the mouse.

My breath became trapped in my lungs, just like my body was trapped between the desk and the hard, hot man behind me. I didn't dare move, not wanting to push him away. I stood still and watched his long fingers move over the mouse and salivated as I remembered how they felt inside me.

My skin vibrated like a live wire as I struggled to keep myself from pressing back against him. If I stood on my toes, I could press my ass directly to his groin. Would I find him hard? Would he stop me?

I was so lost in my fantasy that I almost jumped when his breath tickled against my neck. I closed my eyes, questioning if I was imagining it all—if I was making more out of it than it was. Maybe he wasn't as close as I thought. Maybe he just breathed really hard.

But then my hair shifted, and his heat pressed against my back even though he wasn't touching me. It emanated from him— reached for me. I swayed back but still didn't press to him. I just wanted to be closer.

A small moan crept from my panting lips when his beard gently scraped against the tender skin of my neck. And then a whimper when I heard him suck in a deep breath.

"Cupcakes," he whispered, his deep voice like gravel. "You still smell like the sweetest cupcakes."

I was about to give in, press myself fully against him, dig my fingers in his hair and pull him down so I could turn and kiss him. Only a breath away from snapping.

"Mr. Kent," Vivian called.

Kent stepped away, and a rush of cool air raced to replace his heat, causing chills to spread down my body. I took a moment to collect myself before turning and seeing the expression on Vivian's face. If she saw anything, would she tell Daniel? The idea of Daniel knowing I was practically throwing myself at his best friend, sent a shudder down my spine. I didn't want to see how he'd look at me knowing that. But when I looked over at her, she was walking from around the corner, eyes glued to the papers in her hand. She looked up and gave me the same warm smile she'd given me all day.

"Hey, Olivia. If you're done looking, you're free to go. You've more than met your hours for the day."

"Okay. Thank you so much for all your help." I only briefly let my eyes flick to Kent's, expecting him to be looking away but was instead staring right at me. My glance was too fast to assess what hid in the dark depths, but now wasn't the time to stare no matter how much I wanted to.

"How'd she do today?" Kent asked Vivian.

"Fantastic. You may have to put her on payroll if she keeps helping." I smiled at her wink.

"We'll see what we can do."

And that was the last they acknowledged me, turning to face each other and go over whatever was in Vivian's hand. I took that as my cue to leave and grabbed my belongings from the back offices.

Everyone said their goodbyes and made sure I was coming back again. I had to admit it was nice to feel so accepted.

It also felt nice that as I was walking out, I turned to take one last look at Kent to find him staring at my ass. I stopped, and he looked up to find out he was caught. I wiggled my fingers goodbye and bit my lip to keep from smiling at his tight jaw and twitching mouth.

When I began my exit again, I made sure to add an extra sway to my hips, hoping he enjoyed the show.

No, Kent and I weren't going to have a repeat of our night together, but that didn't mean I couldn't enjoy myself flirting and torturing him with memories.

6 OLIVIA

"If you use the blue painting, it's more calming," I said to Vivian. We were currently staring at a slew of canvases leaned up against one of the lobby walls. "Make sure to place it vertical, it will help draw the eye up, and the room appear bigger. And you know what they say, bigger is better."

I nudged her with my shoulder and waggled my eyebrows, making her laugh.

"I don't know," a deep voice rumbled behind us. "I hear the motion of the ocean is more important."

His voice washed over me, tightening every muscle on its way down to my core. I was on week two of my internship, and I hadn't seen Kent again after our...I didn't even know what it was. Apparently, he'd been in New York with other business.

Forcing the trapped air out of my lungs, I slowly turned. He stared down at me with his dark eyes alight with laughter and a smirk on his lips. I wanted to step into his space and make a seductive joke back and was about to until Vivian playfully slapped his shoulder, reminding me of her presence.

"Stop, Alex. You're going to scare the poor child."

Vivian's attention was on Kent, preventing her from seeing my annoyed side-eye. But Kent saw it, and that devious smirk lifted to a full-on smile. I transferred my glare to him, and his chest shook with a quiet laugh.

"I doubt much could scare Olivia."

Vivian shook her head like Kent was an errant child she had to accept would never change. "How was New York?"

"Productive. We'll have to set up a time to meet later, and I'll go over some of the details."

"We can go now," she suggested. "I'm going to make note of the painting and head to lunch."

"I was actually going to take Olivia to lunch."

My eyebrows slowly rose, confused by the invite.

"James told me she'd been here more than necessary this past week, and I figured I could treat her. Take some time to answer any questions she had." He must have seen the direction my mind was going as I thought of all the dirty questions I could ask, because he quickly added, "For her project."

"Okay. You two have fun, and I'll catch up with you later. Thanks for your help, Olivia." And then she was gone.

"What if I don't want to go to lunch with you?"

"Don't lie, Olivia. You're not good at it."

"You could have at least asked," I muttered.

"Why bother when I know you'd accept anyway?"

He had a point. I was being stubborn because I could and decided to let it go, even if I was having fun bickering with him. "Where are you taking me?"

"It's a surprise."

The perpetual playful tilt of his lips was in place as he stretched his arm out, gesturing for me to walk ahead. Wanting to get back at him for laughing earlier, I walked too close and stopped when my shoulder brushed his chest. Looking up, I put my own smirk in place and spoke in my best Marilyn Monroe voice. "Welcome back, Mr. Kent."

His jaw ticked, and his chest expanded, pressing harder into my shoulder. "Careful," was all he said.

"Never."

And then I walked to the door, biting my bottom lip, trying to hold back the full smile when I heard his growl behind me.

"Who orders just cheese on their pizza?"

"Who orders mushrooms?" Kent shot back. "They're a fungus."

I shrugged and made a scene of taking a bite of my pizza, humming.

He shook his head with a laugh and dug into his own food. We'd been able to walk to the restaurant from the hotel, and it had been silent the entire way. Not that it was bad. It was comfortable as we walked through the streets of downtown, letting the passing cars and people talking fill the silence between us.

"How have you liked the hotel so far?"

"It's good. Better than I thought I'd like it."

His head cocked to the side. "Why didn't you think you'd enjoy it?"

"I don't know. There hasn't been a business that enticed me enough to be excited about it."

"You seemed excited when you first accepted."

I bit my lip and stared out the window, watching people and cars move past. One, two, three people passed before I decided to go for blunt honesty. I turned back to Kent, watching his jaw move as he chewed his pizza. The movement was barely notice-able behind the thick scruff that highlighted his lips.

"To be honest," I began, shifting my eyes to his, just to find him staring at my mouth. When he looked up, he was unrepentant at being caught, setting a flutter of butterflies through my stomach. "It was you I was excited about."

His Adam's apple bobbed around a swallow, and he sat back, pulling in a deep breath. He sat there silent, and I held my breath, waiting for what he would say in return. I didn't mean much by my confession. I didn't mean I had expected anything to happen between us. But the thought of seeing him and feeling the tension strung tight between us had me eager to be around him. And I couldn't have denied myself that after not having felt that same excitement in so long.

He finally opened his mouth, and time stood still.

"Livvie-baby." The nickname was like nails on a chalkboard, especially when Aaron interrupted what I really wanted to hear.

Kent's jaw snapped shut, and he jerked his head to the tall, blond, all American boy walking up to my side.

"Hey, Aaron." I didn't bother to hide my annoyance. "What are you doing here?"

"Just meeting some of the guys for lunch. Pizza on campus is the worst."

The guys walked past him, slapping him on the back as they moved to their table. I expected Aaron to go with them, but he leaned against my booth, licking his lips and staring down like he had a right to look me over.

"Well," I began when it was clear he wasn't moving. "It was good to see you. Enjoy your lunch."

"Yeah, you too." He stood upright, hearing the dismissal. He gave Kent an assessing look, stopping before getting too far and turned to me. "Call me later. Maybe we can meet up for a quickie."

He winked and bolted. Probably because he felt my eyes trying to burn him alive with the rage I had pouring off me. I had to cling to the wood of the table to keep from going after him and kicking him in the balls. He had no idea who Kent was, but what if this was an important meeting and he'd just ruined it. Oh, I'd be calling him later to give him an earful.

"Seems like a nice guy." Kent's tone was hard and sarcastic.

Closing my eyes, I counted to ten before getting the nerve to meet his eyes. He looked like he was holding back his own anger issues.

"Boyfriend?"

I laughed. "God, no."

A slow nod was his only response. When he continued to stare, and the silence turned awkward, I felt compelled to explain and fill the void between us.

"He was a boyfriend a long time ago. But he's a jerk. So, now I just close my eyes and use him for sex."

"Sounds smart." His voice was both bland and condescending.

I couldn't help but feel judged, and it pissed me off.

"Listen, who I sleep with is none of your concern. I choose how much of myself to give, so if my sex-life doesn't live up to your standards, I'm sorry."

When he looked again, the hard glint in his eyes had softened. "I'm not judging you, Olivia. You just deserve better."

That wasn't the answer I was expecting, and it took the wind out of my sails. I relaxed against the cushions of the booth and rubbed my finger along the scratches in the wood. What did I say to that? Honesty seemed to work well the first time, so why not try it again.

"Let's just say I'm not hunting for any mediocre college guys. Not much really compares to my night with you."

I looked up from under my lashes to see his reaction. His eyes heated slowly, but then he blinked, and a wall came down, filtering it to a barely-there warmth.

"You shouldn't romanticize our night."

"I didn't say I did."

"Not really. But you do. I can see it when you look at me."

My hand stopped tracing the grain of the table. How did he pick up on that from the little time we'd spent together?

"You put it on a pedestal and think you want more of that, but Olivia, we can't repeat that night. No matter how much either of us would like. I can't."

Pride swelled in my chest that he'd admitted he would want to sleep with me again. Even if we never did, there was a confidence that boosted my ego just knowing this man wanted me.

When I didn't say anything, he continued his explanation. "It's not just about Daniel. It wouldn't be the same either way."

"Why not?"

"I used a bit of kid gloves with you." Now he was looking up at me from where he'd been staring at his fingers tracing the wood. I didn't ask him to explain, but I hoped my silence would encourage him. "I...have particular tastes."

"Like..." I trailed off, trying to hide my desperation to know more. I held my breath as he stared at me and weighed his words.

"Not what we did that night."

I gave him a hard stare, not hiding my disappointment at his vague non-answer.

A lightbulb went off, and I tried a different approach. "What room would you pick at Voyeur?"

He laughed softly at my victorious grin. "One that would scare you."

This time I rolled my eyes and slouched back into the seat. "Probably not, but if it helps to make me less appealing, then go on believing I don't want to be tied down and spanked."

The words were a guess that rolled casually off my tongue, but I kept a close eye on his reaction. *Jackpot.* His fists clenched on the table, and his whole body grew in the seat as though just the mere mention of the act called for him to be bigger—to be more.

Shit. He wanted to tie me down and spank me. He'd done some light smacks to my ass, but nothing that required me to be tied down. It should alarm me to give up that kind of control. But it didn't. It had me squirming in my seat and almost desperate to make more guesses.

Before I could push anymore, his control slowly slipped back in place, and I watched him relax one muscle at a time. I knew what was coming before he even opened his mouth, and I cut him off before he could slip another denial in.

"Don't worry, Kent. I'm kidding." I waved away my words like I hadn't noticed his heated excitement. "I'm just a nice girl, living out her college years with a sad sex life. At least it will help me focus."

"That sounds like not enough for you."

It wasn't, but I wasn't wasting my time either. Unable to deny his assumption, I simply shrugged. "It is what it is."

Unless something took over Kent's body and he decided to give me a repeat, I was stuck where I was at.

It didn't mean I couldn't imagine.

Closing my eyes, I pretended I could feel rough facial hair against my thighs.

Only now, I was tied down and spanked between wet, sucking kisses.

7 OLIVIA

This time walking into dinner, I'd at least known to expect Kent sitting at the table. Which was why I'd made it a point to clear my schedule and be there. We'd finished out the week with no incident or discussion of our night together. He was polite and business-like. But I caught him staring more than once, and each time almost burned me to ash. Each time he met my eyes after being caught, there was zero remorse, and he'd scan my body again before finally looking away.

There was no doubt Kent still wanted me. But there was also no doubt that he wasn't going to repeat our night. Logically, I knew that was the right decision and didn't pursue it. I wasn't desperate enough to throw myself at someone who would continually turn me down. Too bad, my body didn't get the message.

"Two nights in one month," my mom said to Kent across the table. "I'm liking this trend."

"How can I turn down such good cooking?"

"It's the least I could do for all your help. Usually, David is able to assist me with all my computer woes, but he's still out of town for work."

Daniel slapped Kent's shoulder. "Kent's a whizz with computers. Almost got a degree in computer science before I lured him over with my business plans."

"Biggest mistake of my life," Kent joked, slapping Daniel's back harder.

My mom smiled and shook her head. "You two are grown men, and yet, you still act like boys in college."

They both shrugged, unrepentant with who they were. Daniel had always been a work hard, play harder kind of guy, and I imagined Kent was the same way.

"And I get Olivia here twice in one month too. I really am being spoiled with attention."

"Har. Har, Mom. I'm here more than twice a month." I looked over at Kent, who was looking anywhere but at me. He'd had no problem staring at the hotel, but in my home, he avoided looking at me like I was Medusa and would turn him to stone. "Besides, I can't pass up the opportunity to see my new boss outside of work."

"How is your project going, by the way," Mom asked.

"Good. I'm enjoying it more than I thought."

"I hear you're there more than you need to be," Daniel chimed in. "You going to become a hotel magnate like Kent here?"

Daniel winked, and it warmed me to my bones. He'd always told me I was destined to be great. He said I had too much power within me to be the socialite my parents envisioned.

"I hardly doubt Olivia will run an empire. Maybe a shopping one," Mom joked. My parents loved me and supported me, but like most people, they didn't look past the surface. Not like Daniel did.

"Maybe someday," I said, ignoring her comment. "Who knows, maybe I'll use all of Kent's information against him and start my own empire to challenge his."

He finally looked up and cocked an eyebrow at my challenging stare. His lips parted like he was going to speak when the front door opened.

"Honey, I'm home," my dad called from the foyer.

My mom's face lit up as she stood from the chair to greet my dad when he walked into the dining room. "You weren't supposed to be home until next week."

"I finished up early and rushed home for my girls."

I'd been staring at Kent as everyone's attention was focused on my dad, and his neutral expression tensed when my father kissed the top of my head like I was a child. During our night together, when I'd admitted I was only nineteen, Kent had frozen, and I was sure he was going to pull away. But he'd already tasted me—touched me. My age hadn't mattered past having more. But sitting at my family table with my father, my age sat like an elephant between us, impossible to ignore.

"Speaking of travel," Dad began, settling into his seat. "How was New York?"

"Good," Daniel and Kent said at once.

"We had a meeting with our market analyst at Voyeur a couple weeks ago and feel good about where we're taking it," Daniel explained.

"I'll have to host my next meeting there," Dad joked.

"Kent set it up," Daniel explained, nudging Kent with his elbow. "He likes to mix business with pleasure. No matter where he goes."

My dad barked a laugh while my mom admonished Daniel for talking so openly.

Kent glanced my way only for a second before facing my dad with a shrug and leaned back in his chair like he hadn't a care in the world.

"By the way," Daniel continued, ignoring my mom. "Did you take that woman home that night?"

I dropped my eyes to the table, unwilling to watch his reaction. I ground my teeth, trying to ignore the heavy weight sitting on my chest. I wasn't familiar with the feeling spreading like fire through my veins. But the thought of Kent—of being presented with solid evidence that he'd fucked someone recently—had every muscle in my body tightening, rejecting the idea.

Jealousy. I was jealous.

Such an odd feeling. With Aaron, I'd been devastated, but not this. I'd never had jealousy touch me before as I'd had everything I could want or need. Except for Kent.

"That's enough, *boys.*" Mom made sure they heard her slight by calling them, boys.

"Don't be with men like us, Olivia," Daniel said, laughing at my mom's scowl. Somehow, I managed to lift my eyes and give a semblance of a smile, avoiding looking over at Kent.

"Hardly," I scoffed, earning a proud nod from Daniel.

"You're a queen, and they should kiss your feet," he praised. It was small things that Daniel said that instilled a strength in me. He would always push me for more like he expected nothing less, and I never wanted to lose that. I never wanted to do anything but make him proud, because he was the only person to ask for more beyond being pretty.

Mom made jokes about my obsession with shopping, but it'd rarely been about the clothes and everything about the materials, the colors, the design. I'd find an outfit or a room and think of ways I'd design it to make it better. Mom had stumbled upon my sketch pad and had told me it was pretty. Daniel had stumbled upon me and had sat down and asked me what my plans were to make it a career.

"Don't be with any men," Dad chimed in, pulling me from my thoughts.

My mom scoffed and rolled her eyes before turning to me. "By the way, how was your date with Aaron."

"It wasn't a date, Mom. He's not my boyfriend."

I'd gone over to Aaron's with the intention to ease the ache growing in me each moment I was around Kent. I'd needed a release from someone other than myself. But when Aaron had started kissing me, I couldn't even close my eyes, make a grocery list, and pretend. Much to his disappointment, I'd made an excuse and bolted.

"Good," Dad said. "Let's keep it that way." He slapped the table like he was dropping a gavel on the subject. "Dinner was delicious, Jules."

"Thank you. I'm glad you were able to make it."

My dad looked at his watch. "Well, it's almost nine, which calls for a drink. Kent. Daniel. You two want to come have a drink in my office?"

"Almost nine?" Mom asked. "Oh, shoot. I have a phone call with Linda about the charity meeting." Mom looked at the dishes with a frown.

"I've got clean-up, Mom."

She turned to me with a relieved smile like I'd said I'd donate a kidney and not just some time. "Are you sure?"

"Of course, no big deal."

"Well, we'll help clear the table before heading to the office," Dad offered.

"Thank you. Alexander, it was so good to see you again. Don't be a stranger." She stood and gave us all a smile before leaving.

I gathered the dishes and took them into the kitchen, hearing the chairs scrape back as the guys did the same and piled the plates and cups by the sink.

"You need help?" Dad offered.

"That's okay. Go relax after your long flight."

He gave another kiss to my head and headed to his office. Daniel ruffled my hair before he and Kent followed behind.

Before they left, Kent gripped Daniel's shoulder to get his attention. "I'm gonna run to the restroom real quick." But when he should have gone right to the bathroom, he instead stood in the doorway, watching my uncle and dad until they disappeared. Then he stepped back into the kitchen and turned to face me.

I ignored his stare and focused on rinsing the dishes. I didn't want to meet his eyes and let him see the fire that still simmered in my chest. I peeked from the side of my eye and took in the way he stood tall with his hands shoved into his pockets. He didn't say anything until he was only a couple feet away.

"Did you have a good time with your boyfriend?"

"He's not my boyfriend. And it was fine." I paused when I set the plate in the dishwasher, giving him my full attention. "Why do you care?" I asked like a challenge. Maybe the same heat that singed me at the thought of him with another was burning through him too.

His brows lowered like he was also confused about why he'd asked. Finally, he shook his head and answered. "I don't. It was just a friendly question."

A friendly question?

I snorted at his bullshit answer. He'd stayed back just to ask a friendly question? I doubted it. I closed the dishwasher and stood to my full height, shoulders back like I was preparing for battle. He wanted to ask about my night, so I figured I'd return the favor.

"Well, then, *as your friend*, did you have a good night with your lady-friend at Voyeur?" The fire burning through me intensified as images of *our* night at Voyeur assaulted me. Did he get her off in the hall? Did he use kid-gloves with her?

He pulled his shoulders back to match my pose. We stood like we were preparing for a duel, and I didn't even know what we were battling over. Who would cave first and admit to the jealousy? Who would give in to the tension tugging between us?

"Good enough, I didn't have to close my eyes and imagine someone else."

Everything in me froze and pulled tight like a screw was twisting the muscles in my body. My jaw clenched around the blow that almost knocked the wind out of me. His stance softened when he noticed the hurt his words had caused.

But I didn't want his kid gloves.

I didn't want his pity.

I wanted to land my own blow.

I wanted to make him squirm.

I relaxed my body and licked my lips, knowing I'd already won when his eyes dropped to track the movement of my tongue. "What would you say if I told you I imagined you?" His eyes widened a fraction, and the first drop of victory spread, urging me to go further. "As I sat astride him, I closed my eyes and thought about being tied down and at your mercy."

"Careful, Olivia," he managed to squeeze out past his tight lips and clenched jaw.

I smiled at his warning. I'd only just begun.

Taking a step closer, I continued as if I hadn't heard him. "That when I moaned for it harder,"—I stood right in front of him now—"it was really you hitting me with your belt."

I gasped when his hand shot out and gripped my jaw. Not hard enough to leave a bruise, but enough to assert his power over me. "Stop," he commanded, growling the word.

Instead, I smiled and powered through his grip. "That when I fell to my knees and sucked his cock, it was you choking me like you did that night—stealing my ability to breathe."

His grip was like a vice by the time I'd finished. His chest rose and fell as he stared, his brown eyes almost black over his flared nostrils. The moment stretched to what felt like minutes, and I was sure he was going to shove me away after I'd pushed him too hard.

Instead, I stumbled and slammed into his chest just as his hand jerked my mouth up to his, and he took from me. He took everything. He took the air from my lungs, the moisture from my lips, the thoughts from my head. Leaving in its wake, the thumping desire, pounding like a chant through every inch of me. *More. More. More.*

I gripped his arms and moved my lips as much as I could with his grip still so tight. I took as much control as he allowed me to have and gave everything to him. He shifted until my back hit the counter, and he wedged a leg between mine.

Oh, God. His tongue pushed into my mouth, spreading the spicy flavor of his bourbon against my tongue until it was all I could taste. My head spun like I'd been the one drinking at dinner. My whole world falling to the rough grip he used to hold me in place, and every pounding inch between that led to his leg pressed to my throbbing core. I needed relief.

Without thought beyond easing the ache between my legs, I slid my leggings-clad pussy up and down his thick thigh, the friction lighting a spark that shot through me. Over and over again, I rode his leg, gripping his shoulders for support. Any second, I was going to come. In my parent's kitchen, with my dad and uncle two rooms over and my mom just above us, I was going to explode.

He pulled back, and I gasped for air, almost choking on it when he bit my bottom lip before growling, "I can feel your wet cunt seeping through my pants. Are you going to leave a mark when your pussy comes all over me?"

I closed my eyes and kept moving. My cheeks flushed from a mixture of desire and tension, and embarrassment that I was so shamelessly fucking his leg like a cat in heat. He didn't do anything—didn't touch me beyond his grip on my jaw. Didn't move his leg to help me or shift us so he could feel his own pleasure. Just held me still as I worked my way closer and closer to orgasm.

Just a few more strokes.

"Open your eyes." I tipped a little closer to the edge as I took in his flushed cheeks and swollen lips. "If you can imagine me with someone else's cock in you, then you can look me in the eye and give me your orgasm as you fuck my leg."

My heavy breaths became soft moans, and I bit my lip to hold them back.

"Better be quiet. Wouldn't want Mommy and Daddy to hear their little girl." He pulled me in close and licked my lips, where my teeth were buried in the soft tissue. "Because you are just a little girl, aren't you? Dry humping a grown man's leg, nice enough to let you come on him." My eyes began to slide closed again, but he clenched his hand tighter, and I jerked them open. "Come, Olivia. Now."

I did as commanded and rode his leg harder, digging my nails into his shirt, fighting to keep my eyes open as my cum seeped through my pants and onto his. I barely held back my whimpers as waves of pleasure consumed me.

When the ringing stopped, I slowly pried my hands open but left them softly on his shoulders. His grip had loosened and now cradled my face in his palm, supporting my body with a hand on my hip and his leg still between mine.

I licked my lips about to demand he leave with me now so we could continue this when, from down the hall, Daniel's laughing voice reached us. "Kent, you get lost?"

Kent stepped back like I'd electrocuted him, and I almost collapsed to the floor. I watched his eyes go blank as if a bucket of cold water was dumped over him. He swallowed hard and adjusted his stiff length tenting his pants before stepping out into the hall, stopping Daniel from walking in.

"Just lost track of time talking shop with Olivia," he responded easily, his tone light and unaffected.

I didn't hear Daniel's response as they moved down to my dad's office. I pressed my fingers to my lips like I could hold the flavor and feel of him in longer. My mind raced about what it all could mean. Wondered if it was a moment of weakness we gave in to or if it was a tide turning for us, and more repeats were on the menu.

It was reckless, and against all, we said we wouldn't do, but as I rubbed my thighs together to feel the throbbing pleasure still lingering, I hoped for a repeat.

While I didn't chase men, for another chance with Alexander Kent, I may speed walk to get him.

8 KENT

"WE STILL NEED to put the finishing touches on the rooms on floor seven, ten, and twelve," I said to Vivian. It was Monday, and we were making a list of things that still needed to be completed.

"You should take Olivia around. She's got a great eye for things like that and has been helpful with the small additions to the lobby."

My immediate reaction was, no, I didn't need to be alone with Olivia ever again. Then, I thought about it and decided to take the opportunity to talk to her and clear the air about last Friday night.

Just thinking about it had blood rushing to my cock. It also had me wanting to slam my head on the desk, hoping to knock some sense into myself. I'd never been good at denying myself. If I wanted something, I usually took it. I liked to live my life enjoying the pleasures the world had to offer, and Olivia was a hell of a pleasure the world kept offering me.

My inability to say no to what I wanted had gotten me into trouble before, but nothing compares to how bad it would've been if her family had walked in on me kissing a twenty-year-old girl, who was riding my leg to orgasm. My eyes slid closed, and I bit my lip to hold back my moan. Thankfully, Vivian had turned to work on her computer, missing the sight of me remembering the sweet torture of feeling Olivia's heat seep through my pants, but still not touch her.

I loved watching her move at my command. I loved the way she couldn't look away as my fingers held her where I wanted her. I had control of her body, and I didn't even need to coax her into it. The irony wasn't lost on me that I loved the control I had on others. Like if I controlled them more, then I could be a little more reckless with myself.

"Here she is now." Vivian's voice broke through my daydream, and I pressed up against the desk to hide the way my cock hardened to the point of pain. Watching Olivia stroll in with a sly smirk on her full lips didn't help my case.

I looked at the computer, anything to pull my attention away from her. Taking a drink of my coffee, I focused my attention on the way the hot liquid singed down my throat rather than the young blonde now standing directly across from me.

"Good morning, Mr. Kent. Good morning, Vivian."

I didn't look up as I nodded in response, instead, looking at an ordering receipt like it held the answers to what to do next. Thankfully, Vivian saved me from having to form sentences while the blood slowly returned back to my brain.

"Good morning, Olivia. If you want to set your stuff down, Kent could use your help in the rooms."

"Oh, he does?" Her playful tone had my head jerking up to give her a disapproving glare. She just bit her lip to hold back the laugh shaking her shoulders.

"Yes," Vivian continued, not picking up on Olivia's innuendo. "We have some finishing touches in decorating to do, and you've been so helpful with everything else, I thought you'd be perfect for the job."

54

"I'd love to. Let me just set my stuff down, and I'll be right back."

"Meet me by the elevators," I ordered.

Before heading that way, I grabbed Olivia a coffee.

"Thank you," she said once she'd met me. She smiled, and I tried to find any hint of what she was thinking but found nothing but polite civility. "What floor are we going to?" she asked when the doors slid open.

"Let's start on seven and work our way up."

She pressed the button, and I rolled the words I wanted to say around in my head. Her eyes stayed on the numbers counting higher and missed the way I opened and closed my mouth, trying to start the conversation.

When the doors slid open, she stepped out and turned to face me, amusement sparking in her eyes. "Don't worry, Kent. I'm not going to go stage five clinger on you."

My jaw dropped, and the only thing that fell out was, "What?"

She laughed softly. "I noticed you trying to say something to me in the elevator." She opened and closed her mouth like a fish. My brows lowered in irritation at her mocking expression. "I figured you were trying to say something along the lines of, Friday was a mistake and can't happen again," she said in a deep voice.

That was actually pretty spot on what I was going to say, but even in my mind, I couldn't agree with it being a mistake. But it should never happen again. "It was reckless of me."

She shrugged and drank her coffee like dry humping a man almost twice her age in her parent's kitchen was no big deal.

"I just know you're young and figured you have different expectations."

"I may be young, but I have more maturity than you and Uncle Daniel combined," she scoffed. She softened her tone like she was trying to calm a toddler throwing a tantrum. "Relax, Alexander. It was a good orgasm. Thanks for letting me use your leg for relief. I made all that shit up about sleeping with my ex, so it was much needed."

Then she turned away, leaving me there with my jaw hanging open, knowing I'd been played. I almost wanted to laugh at how easily she'd sparked my jealousy on Friday night, pushing me into action. *Well played, Olivia.*

"Which room should we start in first?" she called over her shoulder. My legs finally decided to start working and followed after her. I led her through the door, and she took in the floor to ceiling windows lighting up the soft grays.

"This is nice. Very open."

"Thank you. I didn't design any of it but had some say in the concept."

"What are you wanting?"

I walked over to an array of paintings leaning against the wall and a desk full of knick-knacks. "I need to decide between these for what I want as decoration."

She moved the paintings around and stepped back to look at each statue, glass bowl, and centerpiece. She'd pause to look around the room again and then looked back at the items, her head turning this way and that like seeing it from a different angle would give her the answer. I leaned back and watched her work. She was careful with each item, and Vivian was right, she looked comfortable.

"This painting here." She grabbed it and moved it behind the lamp on the desk. "It adds color to the neutral feel of the room. But not too much. And then this abstract-flower-looking-statue can go here." She arranged them all and pushed everything else off to the side, standing back to look at her work when she was done. "That way, it gives the illusion of flowers without actually having the hassle of flowers."

I nodded, impressed with her final product. "Okay."

Her head jerked to me. "Okay?"

"Yeah, why not?"

"Don't you need to confer with your designer? A professional?"

"Nah. You seem to know what you're doing. I'm impressed."

Maybe for the first time ever, I saw a smile tip Olivia's lips that wasn't playful and devious. It was soft and paired with the way her shoulders went back, and her chin lifted, she shined with pride. Olivia was a confident young woman, but I couldn't recall a time I'd seen her take pride in her work.

I was unable to stop myself from smiling with her. She looked beautiful.

Standing upright, I nodded my head toward the door. "Come on. I'll show you the other floors."

"Aren't they the same as this one?" she asked, following me out.

"Nope. Each floor has rooms decorated differently."

"That's so cool. People will want to keep coming back until they're able to experience each room."

"That's the plan."

"Your designer is smart."

"That idea was all me."

"Oh, well then, lucky guess." She shrugged but pursed her lips to keep from laughing.

"You're hilarious, Miss Witt."

She bowed as we exited the elevator and went to another room. She entered and spun, taking in the browns, leather, and darker woods, but stopped when she spotted the four-post bed. She turned her head slowly to look over her shoulder, giving me the devious smirk, I was becoming to know so well.

"Did you plan each floor to look like a room at Voyeur?"

I barked a laugh. "Not that I know of."

"Oh, come on. Is this the floor where I get tied up and tortured with pleasure?"

She flopped back on the bed and made an X with her body, her arms, and legs reaching for each post. I laughed again, amazed that this girl could both humor me and turn me on all at once.

She threw an arm over her eyes. "Help," she said in a breathy voice. "I've been captured by a Viking and tied up for his pleasure. I'm too young to have death by orgasms."

"What a way to go," I managed to say through my laughter. I remained glued to the wall across from the bed, not trusting myself to not fall on top of her and take her up on her idea.

She flung her arm wide and lifted her head to give me a serious look. "Where's the gang-bang floor? I want to visit that one."

"Jesus." I rolled my eyes, and my cheeks cramped from smiling so much. Shaking my head, I peeled myself off the wall and headed to the door. "Come on, Damsel in Distress. We have work to do."

Once we made it back to the lobby, Vivian waved me over. "Your tux was delivered from the tailors for the charity event tonight."

"Are you going to the gala for the survivors of human trafficking?" Olivia asked.

"Yes. We make a hefty donation. Part of business is to give back to the town you're in."

"Yeah, it's a local tech company that started the foundation. Mom knows all the local charities."

"Are you going?" My chest thumped at the possibility.

"I thought about it. I needed to see how caught up on homework I could get."

"Well, if you're not too busy with school, you should come as my companion." I took a drink of coffee to hide my wince. Stupid,

stupid mouth opening before thinking. I was supposed to be putting distance between us.

"Mr. Kent," she gasped and put her hand to her chest. "Are you asking me on a date?"

I choked on the warm liquid and coughed, immediately turning to see Vivian's reaction to Olivia's open flirting.

She laughed alongside Olivia, patting her arm like it was a funny joke at my expense. "I think it's a great idea for you to go," Vivian encouraged.

"Maybe I can teach you a thing or two about galas and business, Mr. Kent. I've been attending events since I could walk. I'm a pro."

"I have no doubt."

She smiled wide and turned on her toe. "I'm off to study some spreadsheets with Kyle." She was halfway across the lobby when she called over her shoulder. "Pick me up at five."

Olivia: I'm running a little late. So, I left the key with the doorman. Come on up.

I'D ALREADY LEFT the hotel when her message came through, and of course, I was running early. I'd gotten my work done at the hotel and felt antsy—eager to pick her up. I figured being thirty minutes early wouldn't have been a big deal.

I thought about waiting in the car, but when the driver pulled up to the building, the urge to go in—to see her—overwhelmed me. Maybe we'd have a drink and talk as she finished getting ready. I wanted to repeat the lightness she'd created in the hotel earlier. She'd been funny and carefree, and maybe I wanted to be carefree with her.

I wasn't a serious man by any means. Julia hadn't been wrong when she'd called Daniel and I, big kids. We played and enjoyed life with only the obligations we set upon ourselves, which wasn't much outside of work. But other than Daniel, I was carefree alone, and for that hour in the hotel with Olivia, I wasn't so alone anymore. I hadn't anticipated how much I'd like that. I'd had a serious relationship, but the woman had made demands of me to be someone I wasn't and sucked the joy out of our love.

Olivia infused me with her extra kind of happiness, only spurring mine on more.

So, I told the driver to be back in forty-five minutes and headed on in.

"I'm here to see Olivia Witt. She said there'd be a key for me."

The man at the desk looked me up and down with a raised brow and pinched lips like I was some sexual predator. But he gave me the key regardless.

I laughed when I walked into the elevator and saw Olivia's apartment was on the top floor. I remembered hearing David grumble about his daughter wanting to live in the dorms her first year of college. He'd paced and cursed her stubbornness and claimed it was only a matter of time before she gave in to his offer of the penthouse. I hadn't ever met Olivia at that time, but just watching David run his fingers through his hair while he clutched a tumbler of whiskey let me know she was a spitfire.

I knocked, and when no one answered, I let myself in. "Hello?"

I had no idea where she'd be in the apartment, and I didn't want to startle her since she wasn't expecting me for at least another thirty minutes.

No sound came from the open living area. Looking left and right, I took in the entirety of the apartment except for what lay down the hall. I headed that way, planning on just popping my head into her room to let her know I was there. I knocked on the first door and eased it open when no one responded to find a small office.

There was no response when I knocked on the next door, but when I opened it, I found a room full of soft grays, navy, and white. There were clothes strewn across the bed and a trail of shoes from a walk-in closet to the mirror in the corner. Closing my eyes, I inhaled deeply, sighing when her scent of vanilla cupcakes assaulted me. God, I loved that smell.

A soft moan had my head snapping to the left, and my heart stuttering in my chest. Steam poured from the crack in the door. Obviously, she was showering, and I needed to leave. I'd let her know I was there when she was out. I was stepping back to do just that when another moan slipped into my ears, igniting my blood and pumping it harder to my groin.

I needed to get out of there. I needed my feet to move back.

Instead, of their own will, they moved forward.

Another moan. This time accompanied by a whimper.

The wisps of steam infused with the rich scent of vanilla and coconut swirled around me, her soft sounds calling to me like a Siren. My palm pressed flat against the door and pushed it slowly open.

I took a single step into the hot room and was met with a sink scattered with products, and a mirror. My whole body finally froze like it should have done before I'd even stepped into her room. Before I'd even stepped into this building.

I looked in the mirror that didn't fog up, giving me a perfect view into the shower behind the door. The glass doors were coated with steam, but it didn't impede my view of the pale skin pressed against the shower wall.

Her blonde hair looked darker as it clung to her breasts.

Her blue eyes were closed under brows furrowed in concentration.

Her lips were parted...just like her legs.

She sat on a bench, her head tipped back against the white tiles as her chest heaved, and she worked a purple wand against the folds of her pussy.

She slid the entire length deep inside her and moaned. I gripped my aching cock and moaned with her. I hadn't meant to make a sound. I wasn't sure what I'd meant to do. I think I wanted to do the right thing and back out, pretending I hadn't seen it.

But I'd never been good at doing the right thing.

As soon as the sound vibrated my chest, my eyes shot up to see if she'd heard. Her blue eyes were open and wide with shock when they met mine through the mirror.

Her hands hadn't stopped moving, and I waited, holding my breath for her to say something.

Anything.

And she did.

Locking our fate into place with one single word.

"Kent."

9 OLIVIA

I should've stopped.

I shouldn't have moaned his name.

I should've been shocked and covering myself—ashamed of being caught masturbating in a shower.

But I wasn't.

His eyes singed me through the glass, and electrical power surged through my limbs. My lips parted, and his name fell from them like it'd been waiting there my whole life.

I waited for him to do something—say something. Instead, he stood there frozen, watching me.

Well, if he wanted to watch, I'd give him a show.

I moaned again as I slid the toy through my folds and pressed it inside. I wished it was him. Just like my fantasy.

I'd been chasing an orgasm with the vision of him behind my closed eyes.

But there he stood like my fantasy had been so fierce—*so desperate*—it conjured him before me.

Except, in my fantasy, he rushed to join me in the shower. Instead of standing there, frozen.

I slid the toy out and back in one more time, holding his stare. When he refused to move, I hesitated. Maybe I misread the tense muscles of his body. Maybe I was making a mistake, and he wanted me to stop.

Heat burned my cheeks, and I dropped my gaze as I pulled the toy from my opening.

"Don't." His voice cracked like a whip in the tiled room.

My eyes snapped back to his. He still stood there like a statue, and I had a moment of wondering if I'd imagined his command. Then his body relaxed in increments. His shoulders rolled back. His fists unclenched. His posture softened as he leaned back on the counter, and his lips quirked up on one side.

"Finish for me," he ordered his voice like gravel. "Let me hear your whimpers while you make yourself come."

My heart thundered, rushing blood to my core, creating a pulse so strong I ached to ease it. I slid the toy back inside and held it there, rolling my hips and pressing my thumb to my clit.

"Roll your nipples."

Scooting my butt to the edge of the seat, I spread my legs wide and continued to fuck the toy, giving him the sounds he demanded. My hand slid up my body until it cupped my breast, my fingers moving to roll and tug the hard tip.

Each pinch pulled a cry from my parted lips, and I braced myself for the orgasm about to consume me.

"Tell me what you're thinking."

His voice was like a touch, vibrating across the space between us and rolling across my skin, bringing it to life.

"You," I breathed. I managed to keep my eyes open and watched his fists clench around the counter, his jaw tight. "Inside me. Fucking me. Taking me. Consuming me."

Just speaking about how much I wanted him was too much, and my body caved. My back arched as wave after wave of pleasure crashed over me. My cries rattled against the shower, mixing with the falling water like I was playing a symphony just for him.

My body slowly relaxed, and I tugged the toy from my still spasming pussy, but I didn't move from my position on the bench. I held his stare, almost challenging him to make the next move.

"Come here."

Victory sparked inside me, and I bit my lip to hold back the gloating smile. I stood and turned the water off before walking across the heated tile to him. I didn't bother to grab a towel and dry off, just held his gaze, and strutted over. When I was almost pressed to where he still leaned against the counter, I lifted my hand, wanting to touch him.

Before I could get too far, his hand shot out and gripped my wrist like a shackle. The fast movement shocked me and had me frozen to the spot, eyes wide. The barely reined in desire behind his dark eyes broke free, and a slow smile spread across his lips.

It was the only warning I had before he swiftly tugged me forward, shifting our positions. He pressed me against the counter, facing the mirror, keeping my arm tugged up behind me, between us.

The soft fabric of his slacks rubbed against my bare skin as he pressed his hard length between the cheeks of my ass, fucking me softly. He held my stare in the mirror, daring me to fight him—to tell him to let me go, but that was the last thing I wanted. He could man-handle me all day.

He thought he needed to use kid-gloves with me, but I was ready to show him how much I wanted to take. The hand gripping my wrist pushed against my back, forcing me to bend over the counter. He let me go to grab a condom from his wallet, and my pulse thundered harder.

He was going to fuck me. This wasn't foreplay. This was sex, and I was ready, on the verge of tears because I was so happy. I'd said I didn't need him, and I wouldn't chase him, but god, I hadn't realized how much I'd needed this until I knew it was finally going to happen.

I looked at the stranger in the mirror. My eyes darkened like a raging ocean cresting flushed cheeks, damp from the steam of the shower. My lips were parted—my breaths escaping in puffs to fog the mirror in front of me.

I barely held back a moan when his knuckles brushed against my core so he could unbuckle his pants and slip the condom on. I wanted to push back against him, rub myself on him like a cat in heat, but he had me pinned firmly.

There was no warning before the fat head of his cock brushed my folds, and he pushed all the way in until his balls rested against my clit. He held himself there, his brow furrowed in concentration, his nostrils flared. I couldn't stop myself. I wiggled to get some friction, and his eyes snapped open, a fierce stare telling me he had all control.

A hand snaked in my hair and gripped hard, tugging me until I was upright. My back was arched, my breasts thrust forward. I opened my lips for a witty taunt when he pulled out and began fucking me.

He didn't say a word, making the whole scene that much more illicit. An older man fucking a younger woman in silence, taking what he wanted. All of it made me wetter—more eager to come.

He only gave grunts of pleasure that mixed with my cries. He fucked me like a mad-man, dropping his eyes to watch my breasts bounce with each aggressive thrust.

I needed more of him. I needed him to touch me everywhere, to consume me.

I gripped his hand and brought it to my breasts, demanding, "More. Please."

He leaned down to bite my shoulder at the same time his

fingers gripped my nipple in a punishing twist that had my pussy pulsing hard.

So close. I was so close to coming.

His hand slid up my chest to my neck, wrapping around it like a collar.

"Tap the counter to stop."

The words were so soft, I thought I may have made them up in my need to hear him. But then his thumb and fingers pressed on each side of my neck, choking me. My fight or flight kicked in and demanded I slap the counter in panic, but instead, I locked my eyes with Kent's and focused on the feel of him tunneling in and out of my cunt.

As if my ability to not freak out spurred him on, he squeezed tighter and fucked me harder and harder until I became lost on where he began, and I ended.

Spots danced before my eyes, and my body floated like a balloon. Everything became hazy right before he let go, and I gasped, sucking air as deep into my lungs as possible. It was like I'd sucked a bomb inside my body that detonated. I screamed my pleasure, my whole body tingling and throbbing. I lost myself in the rush of pleasure that intensified more than anything I'd ever felt. I was so lost in myself that I was barely aware of his own moans against my neck.

Our gasping breaths echoed around the bathroom like we'd sprinted through a race. My limbs still tingled, and I would've collapsed to the floor if he wasn't holding me up.

"What the hell was that?" I breathed. He'd given me so much pleasure our first night together, but I'd never felt anything like I had when he'd released my throat, and I'd slammed back into my body just to orgasm.

"Did you not like—"

"Hell, no. It was amazing." I turned my face to his, wanting to kiss him and giggled, light-hearted and euphoric. "If that was no kid gloves, then bring it on."

He inched his face away and gave me a disapproving look, puncturing a hole in my happy place. "Olivia...I can't— We can't—"

I heaved a sigh and looked away but kept my tone as light as I could. "Kent, at least pull your dick out before you tell a girl she won't be having it again."

"Olivia..."

"Shut up, Kent."

I pushed him back until he slid out, and I was able to turn to face him. Not asking for approval, I gripped his face in my hands and pulled him down to kiss me. Surprisingly, he didn't pull back, and I decided to take advantage of his weak morals.

My hands drifted to his softening cock and removed the condom. "I miss the taste of you," I whispered against his lips. Slowly, I slid to my knees, loving the way his eyes tracked my every move. Holding his stare, I wrapped my lips around his cock, rolling my tongue to collect every drop of the cum that still coated him.

"Do you like me on my knees? Cleaning you?"

His hand dove into my hair like he couldn't not be in some form of control, even if he still let me suck and lick as I pleased.

"You know, I do." His admission ripped from him, and I smiled my victory, not bothering to hold it back.

Pulling his softening dick into my mouth one last time, I sucked hard and released him with a pop. "Good." I stood and stepped out from between him and the counter. "Now, I need to get ready, and it's going to take some time since you made such a mess of me." His eyes widened a little at my easy dismissal. Feeling I won something even if it was just hiding how disappointed I was by his quick denial of more, I slapped his cheek lightly and kept pretending. "Go grab a drink and wait for me. There's towels in the hall closet if you need to dry up."

With a quick shove, I got him out of the bathroom, his cock still hanging from his open pants. I shut the door and took only a moment to let the smile slip from my lips and breathe in the hurt. My forehead pressed to the door, and I took stock of the feelings, letting them wash over me. Then I stood upright, shook it off, and got ready.

10 KENT

THE WHISKEY DID nothing to calm the thrum of desire coursing through my blood.

I'd just finished coming inside Olivia, and I was already hard again like some twenty-year-old boy and not an almost forty-year-old man. When I squeezed my eyes closed, all I saw was her tongue laving at my softening cock, just so she could taste my cum.

God, the way she responded to me when I choked her. I saw her want to fight it—to give in to her flight response. But she didn't. She trusted me and trusted the pleasure I gave her.

The pleasure I shouldn't have given her.

But remembering her gasping cries, and her pulsing pussy, it was hard to regret. It was hard to not want to do it again, even when I thought of Daniel.

I took another drink, almost choking on it when Olivia came walking out. "What the hell is that?"

She stopped a few feet away and posed, her smile radiant. "Isn't it great? I worked with a local designer to make it."

"You're missing most of the top," I accused.

The skirt fell all the way to the floor, but the top only had two swaths of fabric that crossed over her breasts, meeting at her neck like a thick choker. A triangle of fabric was missing, baring the inside curve of each breast and most of her stomach. The red material was stark against her skin, making her exposed curves all the more apparent.

Every man would be thinking about feeling that soft skin against their lips, hands, and teeth all night long. I knew they would because it was all that clouded my brain now.

She twirled, her smile growing at my growl. Her back was completely exposed, and when she lifted her arms, the perfect view of the outside curve of her breast taunted me too. How the hell was I supposed to make it through the night without gawking at her breasts, remembering how they'd bounced for me as I fucked her just moments ago?

She'd be beating men away with a stick, and I'd have to watch and not claim her, even though I still had her saliva on my cock.

I took a deep breath, getting my desire under control. I'd given in just this once, feeding the beast. Now, I had to go back to denial. I had to at least try.

"Come on, old man."

"Don't call me that."

"Then get that cranky, old man look off your face."

The long skirt swished around her legs with each step toward me. I held my breath, not backing down from the challenge in her eyes, but also terrified of what she would do. She grabbed the glass from my fingers and finished the contents before giving me a saucy wink and heading for the door.

I was so fucked.

As soon as Olivia got in the limo, she pulled out her phone and ignored my presence. I tried to do the same, but I couldn't stop looking at her. Maybe if I got my fill now, I wouldn't be so compelled to do it at the event.

"Please behave in there, Olivia. You're there as part of Kent Enterprise," I reminded her as we walked up to the large brick building.

"Relax, Kent," she scoffed. "I'm a pro at charity events, and I'm not going to make a scene at a charity for survivors of sex trafficking. I have a little more class than that."

"I know. I just know how you like to taunt me."

She looked to me with a smirk just as we walked through the doors. "You make it so easy."

I sighed and fought to not watch the sway of her ass as she strutted into the room.

"Olivia, you look stunning," Julia greeted us as soon as we walked in.

"Thanks, Mom. You look pretty amazing yourself."

I shook David's hand as Olivia and her mom embraced.

"Good to see you, Kent. Thanks for letting Olivia tag along."

"Of course. It's part of the business, and I figured she could learn a lot tonight outside of a business environment."

"He thinks he's going to teach me how to mingle and shmooze like I'm not amazing at it," Olivia said with a laugh.

"She's always been very good at the social events," her mom praised.

"Hey, everyone," Daniel greeted, walking up with Carina on his arm. He leaned down to kiss the top of Olivia's head. "Hey, kiddo. Where's the rest of your dress?"

"Very funny," she deadpanned.

More hugs and air kisses happened as Carina introduced.

"You ready for the meetings in New York next week?" Daniel asked me.

The ladies had been in a conversation, but at the mention of me leaving, Olivia turned with raised brows. "You're leaving again?"

"Yes."

"But you just got back."

"Nothing to worry about, Vivian will be there."

Carina's eyes flicked between Olivia's concerned face and mine. I did my best to give Carina a blank stare in return but was sure I failed when her lips twitched. "I'll be popping in and can go over some things with you too," she said to Olivia.

"Oh, Olivia, make sure to soak up all that knowledge. You're going to ace this project," Julia said excitedly. "Now, if you'll excuse me, I need to go bid on all these wonderful goodies."

"I'll get my checkbook ready," David grumbled with a smile, following behind his wife.

"Alright, Mr. Kent," Olivia said, pulling her shoulders back, drawing my eye to that alluring triangle of flesh. "Take me around and show me the ropes."

I forced my gaze back to hers and ignored the glint lingering there. She looped her hand through my arm, and we made our exit from Carina's too knowing stare.

I snagged a glass of champagne and explained the various businessmen and women around the room. She soaked up every word and asked questions as we circled. Every once in a while, we'd stop and get caught in a conversation. I was worried at first, despite her assurances, she knew how to mingle, that I'd have to help her through the conversations. But I was wrong. At times, Olivia dominated the conversations, winning over men and women with her laughter and easy questions. She took the information I'd given her and asked after their families and businesses like she'd been working with them for years.

Everyone's eye was drawn to her beauty and the confidence she radiated, and I found myself standing back, letting her shine. At least, until one man kept getting closer and closer, his eyes glued to her exposed curves.

"Olivia," I interrupted the man, not caring how rude I was

coming off. "Let's go bid on that spa day you were looking at." I directed her away with my hand on her upper back, ignoring the desire to stroke the soft skin. She stared wide-eyed as I made our excuses. "Sorry, Charles. We don't want to miss out. Nice talking to you again."

"That was rude," she reprimanded.

"What was rude was how he couldn't stop staring at your tits."

She laughed under her breath, shaking her head. "That's rich coming from you."

We stopped by one of the auction items, and she grabbed a glass of champagne from a waiter walking by. "Drinking?"

"Yes." She cocked a brow and dared me to stop her as she sipped from the glass. "No one really cares as long as you spend your money and don't make a scene. Besides, my birthday is next week. Call it an early celebration. It's not like I don't look old enough to drink."

"Can't argue with that," I mumbled.

She smiled before taking another sip, thankfully, not pushing me on my comment. We walked in silence, perusing all the items up for auction. She'd stop every once in a while, and scribble her bid on a paper, slipping it in the box before moving on to another item.

"So, you're leaving."

"I am."

"Can I message you with questions?" she asked, looking down at a pair of diamond earrings.

The question was light and filled with an innocence I didn't believe for a second. "You can ask Vivian."

She looked up with nothing but sin sparking behind her eyes. "But what if I *need* you?"

I cleared my throat and stretched my neck side to side, my skin feeling tighter and tighter the more she looked at me with that burning fire. Her playful gaze called for me to smile back and play along, to give in to my nature of taking what I wanted.

But at the end of the line was her mom and dad, bidding on their own items. Looking around the room to avoid looking at her, I saw Daniel the next group over. There were reminders everywhere that this wasn't just some one night stand I wanted. This was a young woman that came with consequences.

It was time to be mature—time to keep my playful side under lock and key.

"I'm sure Vivian will be able to provide you with whatever you need."

Olivia's eyes tracked up and down my body. "I assure you, she can't."

Heat flooded my veins, and I clenched my jaw so tight I feared my molars would crack.

"Alexander?" a familiar, soft voice called behind me.

My breath rushed out in relief before I turned and greeted the petite brunette with a smile. "Paige, how are you?"

"Good. Great now that I've found you." She stepped into my space and pressed up on her toes to give a lingering kiss to my cheek.

"Hi, I'm Olivia." Olivia thrust her hand into the small space between Paige and me, forcing her to take a step back and shake Olivia's hand.

"Olivia is interning for a college course as I set up the hotel. She's Daniel's niece."

"Oh, how sweet. That's so nice of you to help Daniel's little niece."

Olivia's body stiffened beside me, and I rushed to move the conversation on, preventing whatever snark rested on the tip of Olivia's tongue.

"Olivia, this is Paige. Her father owns the real estate in New York we're looking at."

"Fascinating."

"I have good news, Alex." Paige stepped into my space again, ignoring Olivia's mocking tone and laid her palm on the lapel of my tux. "I'll be in New York next week too."

"Oh, do you work in real estate too?" Olivia asked.

"No. I'm the CFO for an international company. It's complicated, sweetie."

Olivia looked as though she was on the verge of exploding. Her eyes flicked between Paige and where her hand was still resting on my lapel. I opened my mouth to diffuse the situation when Olivia's face shifted to a bland smile, and the girl who worked the room the whole night came through.

"That's fascinating. I'm sure it's thrilling work."

Paige gave her own bland smile and turned to me again, shutting Olivia out. "Dance with me. If we're going to talk business, at least we can do it while you're holding me. I know how much you like that." She spoke the last part softly, but not so Olivia couldn't hear.

I looked over Paige's head to find Olivia's light blue eyes dark with irritation. If she could burn me with a look, I'd be ash on the ground. I knew what she was thinking, that I'd be fucking Paige next week while I was away. And maybe I would be.

"I'd love to dance. Olivia, you're off duty for the night."

Her chin jutted up, and I took my chance to walk away, ignoring the glimpse of hurt lingering in her eyes.

It was for the best. This was who I was. A playboy who rarely said no to a beautiful woman. Maybe the quicker Olivia learned that, the sooner she'd squash this crush and let me off the hook of our desire.

11 KENT

Apparently, Oaklyn had talked Daniel and Jackson into hosting a surprise party for Olivia at Voy. What better place to celebrate your twenty-first birthday than a bar your uncle owned? There was no way in hell Daniel would let her into Voyeur, so our little side business was the second-best place.

"You've got to be there," Daniel demanded.

"D, I'm not made for a party for teeny-boppers." AKA: I didn't want to watch Olivia get drunk and dance. Actually, I did want to watch her dance, but I didn't want Daniel to see how I wouldn't be able to pry my eyes off her body.

"Tough shit. I'm calling best friend obligations for this."

"Why are *you* going to this?"

"I'm helping Jackson bartend. Also, there will be drinking and boys there. I'm sure as hell not leaving those college boys to try anything."

Yeah, I could get behind ensuring no boys groped Olivia. Not that it mattered because I wouldn't be fucking her again, so she could be groped by whoever she wanted. Who cared that the mere thought had my fists clenching? Who cared that I'd turned

Paige down the other night and went home to jerk off to the memory of Olivia?

God, I was so fucked.

I fought from banging my head on the bar a couple hours later. The room was packed and loud, filled with frat boys cheering each other on, and girls squealing with delight at each other's antics. It all grated on my nerves like nails on a chalkboard. I vaguely remembered having similar experiences in college. I just remembered them as being a hell of a lot less annoying. Probably because I'd been just as drunk as everyone here.

"What do you want?' Jackson asked, tossing a rag over this shoulder.

Jackson had been a performer at Voyeur, but Daniel had always had a soft spot for him, and the kid was a whiz with accounting. His role in our business shifted until he eventually became the third investor in Voy.

"Don't serve that lazy asshole," Daniel interjected, carrying a case from the back. "He can get it himself."

Jackson laughed, used to Daniel and me shit-talking each other.

"Just hand me the bottle, and I'll drink until I forget I'm here."

Another loud shriek rang out from the dance floor, and a laughing girl was thrown over a burly shoulder before being carried around a corner.

"Son of a bitch," Daniel grumbled. "Got to stop these savages from fucking in the back hall."

"Hey, that was you once," I taunted.

Daniel laughed and slapped my back as he walked past. "That's still me. I'm just better at it."

I went back to my drink, and he went to go stop the illicit hallway sex like a prude who didn't also own a sex club.

"She's here," Oaklyn shouted from her perch by the window.

The bar was open to the public but mostly filled with people here to celebrate Olivia. They all gathered near the door as Oaklyn directed. As soon as Olivia's blonde hair cleared the door, the hair on the back of my neck stood on end, and everyone shouted a happy birthday.

Her eyes widened before a beautiful smile stretched her full lips. People greeted her with hugs like it'd been years instead of days since they'd seen her.

When there was a break in the crowd, I caught sight of her outfit and choked on the air in my lungs. She wore the exact same outfit I'd seen her in when we first met at Voyeur almost two years ago. Same silver sequins mini skirt. Same silky cream camisole that hung on her curves, not doing anything to hide the fact that she wasn't wearing a bra. A strip of stomach bared between the two materials, begging to have my hand grip her there while she rode my cock.

Shaking my head, I turned away. If Daniel saw me right now, there'd be no hiding how much I wanted her.

Not even bothering with the glass, I tipped the bottle back and drank.

Ten minutes later, she was three people over at the corner of the bar, taking her first round of shots. She dropped the glass to the wood with a slap and, as if she could feel my eyes on hers, looked directly at me.

Her huge smile softened, shocked at finding me there. Then it tilted up with a whole new kind of happiness that I had yet to see her give to anyone else here. I couldn't have stopped my chest from puffing up with pride even if I'd tried. Nodding, I tipped the bottle as a salute.

Her smile turned predatory as she skirted around the few people between us until she stood in the narrow space between my stool and the next. Not sitting down, just leaning against the bar, causing her breasts to sway enticingly under her slip of a shirt.

"Hey, *Mr. Kent.* Surprise seeing you here."

"You seemed surprised by everyone here."

She opened her lips, and I held my breath, waiting for whatever would fall out, preparing myself for the temptation.

"He's here for me," Daniel interjected.

I faced the bar, stiffening my spine to not turn and look at her. Olivia still leaned against the bar, too close, uncaring of whoever was around. I had to admit, I liked her boldness. If she were anyone other than my best friend's niece, I'd be the man taking her to the hallway for sex.

"Thank you, Uncle Daniel."

"Anything for the princess," Daniel exaggerated with a bow and a wink.

A waitress grabbed his attention and pulled him away, but still, I fought to keep my gaze locked forward. My skin pulled so tight over my tense muscles, and I damn near jumped out of my seat when her small hand rested just above my knee.

"Olivia," I growled my warning.

She, of course, completely ignored it. "How's Paige?"

Paige who?

The way she kept biting her lip and inching her hand higher, I barely knew my own name.

"She's fine," I grunted.

"Any *plans* to see her in New York?"

Her immaturity shined through in that moment, letting her jealousy pour out in a snide voice. It was enough to bring me out of the lusty fog she pulled over me, and I gripped her wrist just before she reached my cock.

"That's none of your business."

Her tendons jumped under my fingers when she fisted her hand in irritation. Good for her. I was being a dick about Paige, and Olivia *should* shove me to the curb. Her lips parted, and I braced myself like I always did with her. But a young jock pressed against her back, leaning down to talk.

"Hey, save a body shot for me later." His hand slid over her waist, where I'd imagined holding her earlier, and a primal roar rumbled deep in my chest.

Olivia watched it all and cocked a brow at my reaction before slowly extracting her wrist from my grip, too subtle for the asshole behind her to notice. When I didn't rise to meet the challenge in her eyes, she pouted before turning her head just enough to smile up at him.

"Sure. Now dance with me."

"Yes, ma'am."

Where was Daniel to prevent this giant caveman from dragging such innocence out on the floor to do those moves? They were practically fucking in front of everyone. She flicked her gaze my way to make sure I was watching, and I quickly averted my eyes and took too big of a drink from the bottle.

"The kids aren't *that* bad," Jackson joked.

"That's because you're still a kid." He was in the latter half of his twenties.

"Yeah, but I'm settled down now with Jake. I'm too content to go out and party. They exhaust me just looking at them. I can't wait to get home and curl up with Jake and watch some sports."

I'd never thought of settling down after college. Life had too much to offer to find a home and lock myself in one place. But I had to admit, hearing Jackson talk about his relationship spurred an itch behind my chest that had never been there before—a need I didn't want to think about.

"That girl is fucking wild," Jackson commented, watching Olivia flit from boy to boy on the dance floor. Even that pencil-dick, Aaron, managed to grab her attention.

When she finally extracted herself from her fan club to head to the bathroom, I'd had enough alcohol to let my reckless side free, and I followed her.

By the grace of some divine interference, the hallway was empty when she came out, and I snagged her wrist, tugging her down to the corner.

"Kent. What the hell?"

Swinging her back to the wall, I rested my hand on the side of her head to corner her. "Having fun?"

Her blue eyes blazed, and her pouty lips puckered, glaring at my overhanded attitude. Olivia liked it the other night when I took control, but she didn't do submissive through the day, and I knew I was pressing my luck with her, just begging her to knee me in the balls.

"Yup." She snapped the p, and I felt it like a lash of the whip.

Holding my stare, she snagged the bottle I brought back with me and lifted it to her lips, taking her own long drink. A little dribbled out the corner of her mouth, and it took everything I had not to tip the bottle over her body and lick every inch, getting drunk off her skin.

"You're a fucking tease."

"I don't know what you mean." All innocence. All a masquerade to torture me.

Gripping her wrist, I shoved her hand against my hard dick. "Yes, you do."

Her back arched, pressing her chest into mine, pinning her hand between our bodies where she began to stroke me. "Then do something about it."

I dropped the bottle, not caring if everything shattered, and pressed my hand between her warm, firm thighs, dragging my fingers agonizingly slowly up to her heat. Her nipples pebbled under her silk top, and I was leaning down to suck them—bite them. When the bathroom door creaked open, and I jerked back.

Thankfully, it was a swaying teeny-bopper and not Daniel or Jackson.

"Come dance, birthday girl," the drunk friend practically squealed. "Then we're doing body shots. Bring the old man with you. He's hot."

I somehow managed to hold back my cringe at her old man comment. Olivia ignored it completely, pulling my chin to face her.

"Take me home, Kent," she almost begged. "Fuck me."

"Fuck," I breathed. Using all the restraint I'd stored up over the years when I never said no, I muttered, "I can't."

Disappointment dragged her face down from the hopeful smile. Her eyes dimmed as though a candle being suffocated until it went out. But just as quickly, she pulled her shoulders back, shrugged, and stepped out from where I pinned her. "Have fun with Paige."

Then she turned and walked away, leaving me with regret and no more bourbon since the bottle tipped over when it hit the ground.

"Only top-shelf liquors touch this skin," she shouted to her friend as she rounded the corner.

There was no way in hell I'd be able to stand by and watch Olivia let some drunk asshole drink liquor from her body. I'd fucking murder someone.

Or I'd end up dragging her out and fucking her in the car.

Best friend or not, I'd lay my claim.

12 OLIVIA

Olivia: Question: Do you think this mirror is a good selfie height?

I SENT the picture I took of myself in the lobby of the hotel. It was a wimpy excuse to message him, but I liked that I could send him a picture and talk to him. He'd been gone all week, and I couldn't help but feel the loss.

Since we had sex, the desire that had always been simmering under the surface started to boil over. All that talk of not pushing him became just that: talk. I was constantly thinking of ways to lure him to me. Any time I pretended I wasn't craving him, I knew I was just a liar.

Kent: What?
Kent: How did you get my number?
Olivia: Vivian gave it to me.
Olivia: And selfies are huge, Kent. Get with the program.
Kent: ...

Olivia: People will take pics of themselves in your hotel and post them to social media. But only if you have good mirrors to take pics in.

Olivia: Like this one...

I hopped out of bed and stood in front of my full-length mirror. As soon as I got home from classes, I'd stripped down to just a T-shirt and panties. I flicked on the lamp by the mirror to make sure he had enough lighting to see my nipples through the thin white material. I turned slightly and cocked my butt out so he could see the bottom curve of my ass peeking from the hem.

Looking it over, I thanked my generation for making me so damn good at selfies and hit send.

Kent: OLIVIA.

Kent: Your uncle is right next to me.

My head fell back on a laugh as I imagined Kent getting the picture and fumbling with his phone to hide it. Then I imagined him tipping it enough to keep it hidden, but so he could still stare at my body. I imagined him at a meeting, getting hard as he remembered everything under my shirt.

Olivia: Tell him it's a business question for my class. I asked Vivian, and she told me to ask you.

Kent: Jesus.

Olivia: See how the lighting highlights my clothes.

Kent: What clothes?

Olivia: I'm wearing panties. Do you want to see?

Kent: What the hell am I going to do with you?

Olivia: I have a few ideas.

Kent: You're being very forward tonight.

Olivia: And I'm not even sorry for it.

Kent: I didn't expect you would be.

Kent: We'll discuss the mirrors when I get back.

Olivia: Okay. When *do* you get back?

Kent: Tomorrow.

Olivia: Yay! I can't wait.

Kent: Olivia ...

Olivia: What? Can't a girl be excited to see her boss?? I'm really excited to talk mirrors.

Olivia: I know how much you love to fuck in front of them. Maybe we should test the bathroom mirrors on each floor for research purposes.

Kent: ... I'm in a meeting. We'll talk about the LOBBY mirrors when I get back.

Olivia: At nine at night?

Kent: A dinner meeting.

Olivia: Oh, is Paige there?

Kent: Yes.

Olivia: Does she like fucking in front of mirrors?

Kent: Goodnight, Olivia.

Olivia: Party pooper.

I dropped my phone on the nightstand and went back to drinking my bottle of wine and watching Netflix.

When the last of the alcohol was gone, and the movie was over, I ached. Despite how much I'd taunted him at the bar last weekend, I never went home with anyone. I never let anyone touch me after he left. Nothing brought my skin to life like he did, and the only person I wanted licking liquor from my body was him.

I looked to the bathroom and remembered the way it felt to

have Kent powering into me. I remembered how I was at his mercy with his hand around my throat.

Tossing my shirt across the room, I flopped back on the bed and slid my hand into my panties.

I hated the idea of him with Paige when all I wanted was for him to think of me. I wanted him to ache for me like I ached for him.

Making a decision, and not bothering to think it through, I snagged my phone off the nightstand and held it over my body. I used one hand to barely cover my nipples and spread my legs. I considered taking my underwear off but didn't want to have my pussy out in the cyber world.

I snapped the pic and cropped to just above my lips and hit send.

Olivia: I miss having you inside me.

WHEN I WOKE the next morning—or more like afternoon—I still hadn't heard from him.

Stupid Olivia.

I berated myself all day for my drunken text.

It was one thing to flirt and another thing to outright announce how much I missed him. I just hated the thought of him with stupid Paige. And I hated that I hated the idea.

I was Olivia Witt. I didn't do jealousy. I didn't care enough. I fucked who I wanted, when I wanted, and didn't chase anyone.

The whole day I felt like I was at war with myself. Two parts of me would argue each side.

Obviously, he wants you. He just needs a little push. It's okay to push.

You do not chase anyone. Ever. Don't degrade yourself like that. Don't make yourself that available to anyone.

But the sex with him is so good. I haven't felt this kind of excitement over anything in so long.

Don't let him have that kind of power over your emotions.

I was so tired of being in my own head that when Oaklyn invited me to dinner, I jumped at the chance. Then when Aaron called a few minutes after, I invited him too.

"Why the hell did you invite him?" Oaklyn grumbled when Aaron walked away to use the restroom.

I chewed my cheek, trying to decide how much I wanted to admit. But it was Oaklyn. I told her everything. Maybe she could help settle the internal mess my mind was.

"I sent a dirty pic to Kent and told him I missed him." Her eyebrows rose slowly into her hairline. "He didn't respond, and now I feel stupid. I need to soothe my ego with male attention."

"I'd hardly call Aaron 'male'."

"You know what I mean."

"I do. And only because I know how big of a deal that message was, will I not comment on Aaron again. At least for tonight."

Aaron came back from the bathroom, and Oaklyn even tried to force a laugh at his stupid jokes. I scraped my fork through the alfredo sauce, clinging to my plate, barely listening to him ramble on. I almost jumped out of my skin when his hand landed high on my thigh and moved under my skirt. I slapped my hand over his to stop his ascent. He leaned in and pressed a kiss to my neck, making me cringe.

"Come on, Livvie-baby. Let me get you ready for tonight."

I looked across the table at Oaklyn, who was looking down at her plate but also making gagging motions.

This was a mistake.

I was torn between pushing through with Aaron, just to

prove I could, and pulling back because I didn't want anyone else's hands on me other than Kent's.

My phone vibrated, and I breathed a sigh of relief at having a reason to pull back. I pushed Aaron's hand away and grabbed my phone.

Kent: Meet me in room 1469. Follow the directions.

My heart thundered so hard it blocked out all other sound. A rush of adrenaline flooded my veins, causing an excited tingle from head to toe.

"Olivia," Aaron said loudly like he'd said it before, and I hadn't answered.

"I have to go." I didn't even wait for a response. I threw money on the table, mouthed an apology to a wide-eyed Oaklyn, and got the hell out of there.

I was almost running by the time I hit the door of the restaurant. I snagged a cab and tried to do breathing exercises in the back seat to calm my racing heart.

I took a deep breath at the front door of the hotel and walked in with a calm I was far from feeling. Only a few workers lingered in the lobby, and I gave a polite smile, walking to the elevators like I had every right to be there.

I swiped my master key and held my breath as I pushed the door open. Would he be waiting for me? What were the directions? What would I find on the other side of this door?

I found nothing. The room was empty, and I exhaled hard. Shaking off the disappointment of him not waiting for me, I quickly scanned the suite, looking for his directions.

When I walked into the bedroom, I spotted a large box on the bed with an envelope resting on top. My hands trembled when I unfolded the note.

Strip naked and put on what's in the box.
Follow the directions and wait for me.

I slowly lifted the lid like I'd find a bomb inside.

But I definitely didn't find a bomb, even though what I found made my heart feel like it might explode.

I told him I didn't want his kid gloves.

And he'd definitely taken them off.

13 KENT

STANDING outside the hotel room door, I inhaled deeply, trying to prepare myself for what I'd find on the other side.

I knew she'd be there. I watched her walk in from where I sat in one of the offices off of the lobby. However, I didn't know if she'd follow the directions. I didn't think she'd balk at the plans I had for her tonight, but Olivia was her own woman and one that didn't necessarily bow down to a man. Which made any time she did, a heady, powerful rush.

I'd given her thirty minutes to prepare. Thirty minutes to wait for me. I wanted the anticipation to build. I'd *needed* thirty minutes to gain a little composure. As soon as I'd seen her walk through the doors, I'd wanted to pin her to a wall and fuck her into oblivion.

I still did.

After jerking off to her picture from last night three times, I was ready to say fuck it and give in to the temptress. I was done with this bullshit of denying myself. It stressed me out, and I had enough shit I had to rein myself back on. I was done holding back from burying myself inside Olivia, and frankly, my arm was tired.

I was almost forty, not some teen who imagined what he wanted and came into his hand. I had a willing pussy on the other side of this door, and I was damn well going to take it.

Again, and again.

There was nothing wrong with consenting adults. Daniel didn't need to come into the decision at all. He didn't need to know. He'd never been informed of my sex partners before; he didn't need to know now.

Shoulders back, I swiped my key and entered. Her sweet vanilla scent hit me, and my cock throbbed harder. Staring out at the sparkling city lights beyond the living room, I listened for any sound. A brush of fabric came from the opened bedroom door, and I braced myself for what I'd find.

The most beautiful sight I'd ever seen greeted me.

A moan building deep in my abdomen rumbled up my chest and fell from my lips. Soft flesh pressed to the fluffy white comforter, spread for my taking. I stared at her red-tipped toes, the black, satin cuffs strapping her to the bed, up her slim, spread legs. My mouth watered at the glimpse of her pink pussy, and I fought another groan at her heaving breasts, pulled high from her arms stretched overhead, and cuffed in the same black satin.

What I wasn't prepared for was her red lips pursed in irritation and her eyes a fiery blue.

"You made me wait long enough, Kent." She snarled my name and cocked a haughty brow. God, I was going to love making her bend to my will.

Pushing down the pulsing throb urging me to take, take, take, I gave her my best, unaffected tone. "You need patience, Olivia."

"I need you to fuck me. Not be tied down and wonder if you'd actually show."

"You could have unstrapped yourself." The cuffs that bound her hands were looped through the headboard and had plenty of room to undo the Velcro chaining her in place.

Her gaze narrowed, and her lips remained firmly closed. She may be snapping at me, but I knew if I dragged my finger through her folds, I'd find her wet and wanting. She was a spoiled little girl, not used to waiting—always getting her way. The fact that she went against her natural instinct and waited for me, flooded me with pleasure.

I walked to the bed and rested my hand on her foot. That small touch pulling a gasp from her. I dragged my fingers lightly up her leg, teasing as I explained the rules.

"I've been indulgent, Olivia. I may be carefree and easy-going in my day-to-day, but in here, you obey." Slipping my fingers between her thighs, I rubbed one through her wet slit and rolled her clit under the rough pad. "You will bend to my will."

She moaned and thrust up, trying to gain more friction than I was willing to give. I immediately pulled away, resting my hand on her thigh.

"If you have a problem, simply say red, and we'll stop and talk about it. But until that word slips past your succulent lips, you are under my control."

She remained silent; her mouth still clamped shut. I raised a brow in question, letting her know I was expecting a response.

"Yes."

"Good girl." I patted her thigh and turned to grab a chair. "Now, let's begin."

She tracked my movements and furrowed her brow in confusion when I sat the chair at the foot of the bed and began opening my pants.

"What are you doing? Aren't you going to fuck me?"

"Not if you keep questioning me," I answered, settling back and freeing my cock, giving a few long strokes.

"Kent." Her voice was shrill and panicked.

"Shut up, Olivia." I groaned when I cupped my balls and squeezed my dick harder, my eyes taking in every inch of her exposed body. "I need to prepare you, and right now, all I want to do is fuck you as hard as I can and lick up your tears. I need to take the edge off. Now be a good girl and spread your legs more. Show me your pussy."

After a moment of hesitation, she bent her knees as much as possible and spread her thighs wide, showing me every wet, pink part of her. I didn't tease myself or drag it out, I just needed to come, so I could take my time enjoying her. It only took a minute or two to bring myself to the edge. When I was about to come, I moved to the bed between her thighs. I wanted to see my come splattered on her skin. I wanted to mark her in every way a man could.

She arched her back, thrusting her breasts up, and I groaned my release. My orgasm ripped from my body, hitting her neck, her breasts, her stomach. When my muscles finally relaxed, I fell over, supporting myself with one hand and wiped the remaining cum clinging to the head of my cock on her skin.

"Look at you," I rasped. "My own perfect canvas."

She squirmed under me, and I smirked. I loved how she couldn't hide her ache—how desperate she was for me. I flattened my palm to her stomach and smeared my cum into her skin, leaning down to lap and suck up any drops that coated her breasts. I bit her nipple, letting her moan wash over me.

I dragged my finger through the remaining cum on her neck and brought it to her lips. She didn't hesitate to open and suck every drop.

Keeping my eyes pinned to hers, I moved my wet finger between her legs, skimming past her pussy to press between the cheeks of her ass.

"Has anyone touched you here since I last played with this tight, little asshole? Have you shared this with anyone else?"

She squirmed when I brushed my finger back and forth. "No," she breathed.

"Good. I like that it's mine." I played between her cheeks, loving the feel of her wet pussy leaking down to coat my fingers. She tensed when I pushed my finger in to the first knuckle. "You're going to need to relax if you want to make it through the night, my sweet Olivia."

Her eyes flared with fear, but she didn't stop me as I pushed in more. As much as I wanted to play with her backside for hours, I had plans. I shifted off the bed and grabbed lube and a small plug I bought just for her.

"Kent?"

"'I told you, I needed to prepare you. Do you want me to stop?"

"No. Please."

I coated my fingers and the toy with lube, tossing the bottle aside. My fingers moved back to her opening, and I dropped between her thighs, burrowing my tongue as deep in her tight cunt as I could, while I pressed my fingers inside her ass.

"Oh, my god," she cried.

That was the last intelligible sound she made. I lapped at her pussy, biting her clit, sucking her folds. All while I scissored my fingers in her tight virgin ass. When I felt like she was ready, I pressed the plug against her and eased it in, past her tight ring.

She was just about to come by the time I got it settled and pulled back, standing from the bed.

"What?" Her eyes shot open, wide, and panicked. "No. Please. Kent, please."

"God, I could listen to you beg me all night."

"Kent." Her plea bordered on hysteria.

"Would you like to say your word?"

Her jaw clenched, and her desperate eyes turned a little murderous. "I'd like it if you'd fuck me."

I gave her a serene smile and stripped my shirt over my head.

While her eyes were glued to my exposed chest, I set a small box on the nightstand and moved to release her arms.

"What are you doing?"

"Moving you to where I need you. Now stop asking questions, or I'll say red."

Her eyes dropped to my cock, still hanging from my open pants, already hardening again. "Aren't you going to get naked?"

"Soon. I don't need to be yet."

She grumbled but didn't fight as I sat her up and moved behind her, tugging her back between my spread legs. Her warm skin pressed to my cock, and I gave in to the desire to thrust against her. The view looking down over her shoulder had me almost abandoning my plan and lifting her up, so I could bury my length inside her and come again.

But I had a plan and needed to stick to it, so I could get in her tight ass tonight.

"Don't lose that plug, Olivia."

She tensed like she was squeezing her muscles to hold it in tighter. My fingers slipped between the folds of her pussy, pressing softly but not enough to let her come. Then with one hand still between her legs, the other rolled her nipple, loving the way her juices coated the pale pink tips. They pebbled beautifully, and I reached over for the small box, pulling out what I needed and putting them in place before she could react.

"What the fuck?" Olivia shrieked, trying to jerk forward. She looked down at the small metal clamp encasing her rosy tip.

"I wanted to see you decorated with my jewelry, and since I can't exactly pierce them myself, these clamps will have to do," I explained as I tightened the toy. When I was finished with the other side, I brushed my thumbs across the hardened tips. Her whimpers rang like desperate pleas, and I loved every one.

Moving my hand back between her legs, I began working her back up to come.

"Listen to you," I growled against her ear, shoving my fingers deep and twisting them. Her pussy made vulgar, wet, sucking sounds that shot straight to my dick. "Listen to how wet you are for me. You love being stuffed, pinched, and teased."

"No," she breathed, her head rolling back and forth along my shoulder.

I pulled my fingers out and smacked her cunt hard. She cried out but didn't stop me.

"Don't lie to me, Olivia."

I smacked her again and again.

"I bet all those boys you've been with can make you come by fingering you." *Smack.* "Maybe they've even tongued your little clit until you screamed." *Smack.* "But have you ever come by having your pussy spanked?" *Smack.* "To the wet sounds of a hand hitting your sopping cunt?"

Smack. Smack. Smack.

"Oh, god. Stop. Please."

I paused, giving her a chance to say red. But she didn't. She continued to roll her hips and search for my touch.

"No." I bit down on her lobe and continued to land blow after blow, stopping every once in a while to role her tiny clit between my fingers.

Her whole body tightened, and her lips parted in a silent scream as her pussy spasmed against my hand. I circled her bundle of nerves and helped her ride the wave of her orgasm, telling her how beautiful she was when she came, how hard I was for her.

When she finally came down from her high and her body sagged against mine, I kissed up her neck to her ear. "I'm gonna take your tight little virgin hole now. Will you give it to me?"

"Yes, Kent. Anything."

"I won't be nice," I warned.

She rolled her head so she could look up in my eyes. Hers were half-lidded and glazed with pleasure. "Take it."

I didn't need any more encouragement than that. I moved out from behind her, laying her back against the pillows. Quickly, I stripped out of the rest of my clothes and grabbed a condom before freeing her ankles.

She looked like a desperate virgin sacrifice. Her blonde hair spread out on the pillow, a blush staining her flesh from her chest to her cheeks. Her nipples red and rosy pinched between my clamps. I watched her face as I slid the plug from her ass. She didn't fight me, just parted her lips on a gasp when it slipped free.

I held my breath and rolled on a condom. As much as I said I wouldn't be nice, I wasn't going to rut into her on the first shove. I wanted her to like it because if I continued fucking Olivia like I wanted to, I wanted her to beg me to be in her asshole as much as possible.

Pressing my cock to her tight hole, I eased in slowly, loving the look of wonder on her face—loving the way her lips formed a perfect O when I pressed all the way in. I only gave a few more gentle strokes to let her get used to me before I picked up the pace, desperate to watch her breasts bounce from my aggressive thrusts.

Her cries grew louder, and my balls pulled tight, desperate for release. As much as I was torturing her, I was torturing myself too, and I needed to come. I continued to fuck her, and pulled one of the clamps free, quickly replacing it with my lips. The rush of blood to her tip and my sucking mouth set her off, and she screamed as her ass squeezed me tighter than I'd ever been before. While she was still coming, I moved to release the other clamp, spurring on another spasming scream.

It was too much. All the blood rushed to my dick, and my head swam as I fell over the edge and came. I rutted against her like an animal, spilling every bit of cum into the condom, wishing it was her tight hole I was painting with my seed. I wanted to mark her inside and out. I wanted to make her mine more than anything.

When the flood of adrenaline slowly seeped from my body, I pressed my sweaty forehead to her damp chest and tried to catch my breath.

Fuck, that was the most intense sex I'd ever had. And that was saying something.

I kissed across her breasts and sucked her nipples, slowly easing out of her.

She didn't say anything as she watched me remove the condom. Her gaze sleepy and sated, but still, a fire burned behind them. I knew if I wanted to fuck her again, right now, she'd let me.

I moved up the bed until my cock was by her mouth. "Clean me."

Without hesitation or question, she rolled to her side and ran her tongue all over me, getting every spare drop of cum clinging to my softening cock. When there was nothing left, I pulled back and shifted us until we were beneath the covers. Pulling her into my arms, I brushed her hair back and kissed her everywhere I could reach.

"You did amazing. I'm so proud of you."

"Please tell me we can do it again."

"We'll talk more in the morning, but I'm not done with you."

She yawned and burrowed against my chest. "Good."

"You did so well, Olivia. You're such a good girl for me."

A good girl, I didn't plan on giving up.

14 OLIVIA

I took stock of my surroundings before opening my eyes, fully prepared to wake up alone with another note that thanked me for a good night.

Instead, warmth pressed against my back, and soft puffs of breath caressed my neck. A heavy arm draped over my waist, his hand cupping my breast possessively. Heat that had nothing to do with the man behind me bloomed in my core, remembering what those hands had done to me last night. I shifted my body and smiled at the twinge in my ass. God, that had been so intense. I didn't think anything could surpass our first night together, but Kent took me places I hadn't known existed.

A part of me wondered if I should feel shame at the dirty things we'd done.

But I didn't. I felt everything opposite of shame. I felt pride at the pleasure my body gave. I felt happiness and excitement at the idea of doing it again. It'd been too long since this wave of euphoria—of looking forward to something—had washed over me. The last two years, I'd been checking boxes and moving through life bored.

I wanted to cling to this new feeling as long as I could.
Shifting out from under his arm, I tried not to wake Kent.
Not yet, at least. I froze when there was a break in his breathing,
but he just moved to his back, still asleep. Tugging down the
sheet, I barely contained the moan at seeing his body. Kent may
have been a thirty-eight-year-old man, but his body was delicious.
I barely resisted dragging my tongue along each ridge in his
abdomen, wanting him to wake buried in my mouth and not
being teased by my kisses.

My ass clenched tight when I bared his length. I couldn't
believe I had something so big inside me. I couldn't believe how
much I liked it and how much I wanted to do it again. I made
room for myself between his legs and gripped his shaft, not
wasting time with teasing kisses and diving down as far as my gag
reflex would allow.

On my second pass, a groan rumbled in his chest and a hand
buried in my hair. I worked him hard, sucking even harder.

"Fuck, Olivia," he moaned.

His hips thrust up, chasing my mouth, and I cupped his balls,
rolling the smooth skin in my palm. Another groan and then the
hand in my hair clenched tight, halting my movement. Tears
burned the backs of my eyes from the stinging in my scalp.

"Slow down," Kent ordered.

He kept my mouth on him and moved me slowly up and
down his shaft. When he would hold me up until only the head
rested in my mouth, I would roll my tongue along the back, slip
through the tiny slit, moaning at the salty fluid I'd collect there.

"Look at you." His voice was like gravel, and I was desperate
to see his face.

I looked up, and my pussy tightened at the fire burning in his
eyes. His jaw was clenched, and he looked on the edge of his
control. He pushed me down again, harder this time, and I broke
the stare, needing to focus on the task at hand.

"Look at you sucking my cock. Those pretty little lips wrapped tight, desperate to taste me."

He pushed down too far, and I gagged, pulling a grunt from him.

"Breathe through your nose, sweet Olivia. I want to feel your throat squeezing my dick."

I did as ordered, and tears leaked from my eyes. He held me there, and I forced myself not to jerk back. I gasped for breath when he pulled me off, but I was quickly shoved back down. His thumb wiped away the wet tracks on my cheeks.

"So, fucking sexy," he breathed. "Finger yourself, Olivia. Finger that little pussy and moan around my cock when you come."

I did as told, and he repeated the process of holding me down and lifting me up to get my breath and lick at his length. Each time my lips touched his groin, and I was sure he wouldn't let me up, and I'd pass out, my pussy would get more and more wet. The tension pulled tighter and tighter until I brushed past my clit one last time and did my best to scream my pleasure around him.

"Oh, fuck, yes," he gasped.

He pulled me up and held me in place, putting both hands on either side of my head and fucking up into my mouth. The orgasm ripped through me, an endless wave of pleasure. I couldn't focus on sucking him anymore, but it didn't matter, my mouth was open, and he used the hole I so willingly offered.

He held me down one last time and let loose a roar that rippled through me as he came down my throat. I think, in that moment, I could have lived with his cock in my mouth if it meant this pleasure was mine forever. Not just the aftershocks of my orgasm, but the pride at being able to make such an experienced man lose control and make those animalistic noises. I'd be completely willing to serve at his pleasure for as long as he'd take me.

"Such a good girl, Olivia. You suck my cock so well."

His praise was breathless, and his hand smoothed over my hair like he was petting a cat. I lapped at his smooth length, cleaning any last remnants of his cum and relished in his praise.

"You make me come so hard, baby."

Kissing up his body, my tongue played in the grooves that tempted me before. When he'd had enough, his hand wrapped around my neck and tugged me to him so he could feast at my mouth.

"I love the taste of myself on you." I smiled like a Cheshire Cat. "Now, let me take care of you."

Taking care of me apparently meant a bath, which was glorious on my aching muscles. He left me in the tub to soak as he took a quick shower and dressed. I felt every one of the seventeen-years between us when he stood over my naked body in the tub. Him in his slacks, rolling up his sleeves over tanned, muscular arms. The wrinkles around his eyes and the salt in his dark hair. I felt like a little girl at the mercy of this man, and I loved it.

He took his time to wash my hair and body. Taking care to use his fingers against my cunt, delivering a swift, explosive orgasm before letting me out and wrapping me in a robe.

"Come. I stocked the mini-fridge with food for this morning. It's no gourmet breakfast, but it will give us fuel for the day."

I leaned against the doorjamb as he laid out various fruits, pastries, and yogurts. He'd even brought orange juice and champagne. When he sat back in his chair, I walked to the opposite side of the table to my own seat.

"No," he said before I could sit. I jerked my eyes to him, and a thrill rippled through me when he patted his thigh. "Come here."

I almost ran to him, throwing myself in his lap, but stopped. I loved every moment of being docile for this man, but I was still me. Still me, who didn't run and jump to for any man, no matter how many orgasms. Even if I was going to give in, I still wanted the excitement of the challenge. His jaw clenched when he saw my smirk slowly spread across my lips.

Climbing atop the table, I held his stare and crawled across. My breasts swayed with each move, and I loved the way his eyes dropped to watch. When I finally reached his side, he leaned forward and gripped my jaw.

"You're so fucking sassy, aren't you?"

"You like it."

He grunted and leaned forward to nip at my lips sharply. "I do. Now get on my fucking lap so I can feed you."

I managed to not knock anything over when I got off and perched on his lap. He kissed up my neck and stroked my arms, lulling me to relax against him.

"What do you like?" he asked in my ear.

"Everything," I sighed.

He nipped at my ear, pulling me out of my haze. "I meant the food."

Smiling, I pressed a quick kiss to his lips. "I'm not picky."

It was a little odd to be sitting on his lap and having him feed me when there were five other chairs at the table, and I was a grown woman, but it was also relaxing and felt right.

"Tell me about school," he said, placing a ripe strawberry past my lips.

"Good. Boring. How's work?"

"Good. Not boring. It's why I like my job. It keeps me busy with new things—new places." He smiled and nipped my jaw. "What do you want to do after college?"

Wasn't that the million-dollar question. "I don't know. Something not boring." I sighed, frustrated with not knowing what I wanted yet. "Nothing interests me so far. Maybe I'll just become a socialite." Placing my fingers under my chin, I bat my lashes.

"I'll shop all day and go to clubs for money. Maybe attend charity fundraisers."

"Yeah, right," he said, laughing. "You're too smart for that." Warmth sunk deep in my chest at his compliment. "You're good at the design aspect of the hotel. Vivian tells me you always have great ideas that they use—good marketing ideas. Carina keeps telling me she's going to steal you from me."

Tucking my chin to my chest, I smiled. "I do love designing all kinds of things—fashion and interiors."

"You mentioned your dress, which I still think was lacking some material."

"You loved it."

"Too much," he growled. "Did you decorate your apartment?"

"And Daniel's."

"I'm impressed but not surprised. I'm glad you get to use that skill set at the hotel. Pretty cool place to intern, huh?"

"I guess it's okay," I answered with forced reluctance. Honestly, sometimes, I went into the hotel and couldn't tell if the excitement was the work or the idea of being around Kent.

He popped another chunk of fruit in his mouth and smiled up at me. His eyes were a beautiful brown, so much lighter with the sun shining through the large windows. They matched his mood, and I could get lost in them for hours.

"Kent, what are we doing?" I almost whispered the question.

"Eating," he answered easily.

"You know what I mean."

"I don't know." His answer was quick before popping another bite in his mouth and moving on. "What do you want to do today?"

I pursed my lips and gave him a serious stare, not letting him off the hook. The light brown dimmed as he became more serious and stroked my cheek. I wanted to sink into his touch, but now that I'd asked the question, I needed the answer. I couldn't believe the words had slipped out in the first place. Oaklyn accused me more than once of being a commitment-phobe, and here I was, asking for clarification.

I boiled it down to just needing to know if I'd get to feel more pleasure. This had nothing to do with commitment or the warm goo sliding around my chest.

"I like you, Olivia. I like fucking you. You make me laugh, and you make me come. Two of the most important things to me."

"I like you too."

"Then let that be enough."

Enough.

The answer felt tenuous and fleeting like it could be taken from me without notice. Warning bells jingled softly, a quiet reminder that if I continued down this path of being with him, sitting in his lap and laughing with him, I could put myself in a position I hadn't been in since Aaron. One I'd made sure not to be in for the past two years. Shoving the ominous siren down, I told myself to take advantage of all the pleasure while it lasted. I could spend more time with Kent, give my body to him again and again, and still stay separate.

I'd be the mature woman I wanted to be with him. Not the girl who had old fears and scars clinging to me, making me whiney and scared. It wasn't me. He was mature, and I wanted to match him—be his equal.

"Okay."

His broad smile had me smiling too. How could I not when he looked so happy like he didn't have a care in the world?

"Good. Now, what do you want to do today? I'll give you my whole day because I have to leave again tomorrow."

The smile dropped from my face, just like my heart dropped to my stomach. "What? Again?"

His brows furrowed at my reaction, and I berated myself.

Don't be clingy. Don't be clingy. Be a mature woman. Who cares if he leaves? You are Olivia Witt. Your emotions are not at the mercy of some man giving you attention.

I tipped my lips and lowered my lids to a seductive stare, wriggling on his lap over his cock. "Well, that sucks. I will sure miss you, Mr. Kent."

"Then, let's make today count."

15 OLIVIA

"You did what?" Oaklyn whisper-yelled across the table. We were in a private room at the library, studying, but the door was still open.

Not liking her judging tone and narrowed eyes, I lifted my chin in defense. "Don't judge me. You're living with your professor."

"He's not my professor," she ground out between clenched teeth. "And he's also not old enough to be my father. Also, Callum isn't a relative's BFF."

I shrugged her arguments off. "Yeah, but all Kent's experience is so good. It may never happen again. He was very vague."

Her jaw dropped, and she stared at me like I'd just told her I'd been probed by aliens.

Hardly.

I'd been probed many times by Alexander Kent. My lips twitched into a smile, remembering our weekend. We'd had plenty more sex, christening as much of that hotel room as we could. But we'd also laughed so hard we'd cried. He'd gone out and bought games. We played strip Twister—a game I was sure he made up—which of course, led to sex. So much delicious sex.

"Stop looking at me like that," I demanded, schooling my features into something serious.

She blinked a few times, sitting back and looking at me like she was seeing me for the first time. Any argument she'd been preparing for a moment before vanished as she studied me. "I just can't remember the last time I saw you smile like that."

"Like what? I smile."

"Yeah, just not like that." Her smile was slow, and I braced myself for whatever put that gloating look on her face. She leaned forward, resting her elbows on the table and pointed an accusing finger my way. "That's how I smile when I think of Callum."

I scoffed, brushing off any insinuation that I smile about Kent the way she smiles about the love of her life. "Then why aren't you congratulating me on my happy sex smile?"

She rolled her lips between her teeth, thinking over her words, but the knowing look was still there. The one that said she knew something I didn't. The longer she looked, the more I didn't want to know.

"You like him," she declared.

I scoffed. "Of course, I like him. It's really, really good sex. But it's *just* sex."

She opened her mouth to share her thoughts when a knock came at our door.

"Hey, Livvie-baby."

By a miracle, I was able to hide my scowl at seeing Aaron appear, his nickname grating on me like nails on a chalkboard.

Oaklyn wasn't as successful in holding back her scowl, in fact, she even let a sound of disgust slip free. "We're busy, A-a-ron."

I bit back my choked laugh as Aaron scowled at Oaklyn. He hated that nickname, which meant Oaklyn used it as much as possible. However, he let it slide, sitting in the chair next to me, scooting close enough to toss his arm around my shoulders.

"Livvie wants me here," he said to Oaklyn, before turning to brush his nose along my ear. "Don't you, baby?"

I really didn't.

The thought should alarm me. I'd messed around with other guys and never had an issue when I'd meet up with Aaron again to fool around. I wasn't exclusive to anyone—it was safe that way. But after my night with Kent, Aaron's touch sent a wave of dread washing over my skin.

"Actually..." I shrugged my shoulders to dislodge his arm. But before I could continue, my phone vibrated on the table.

Kent.

"It's the guy I'm interning for," I explained, fumbling the phone in my rush to pick it up. I cast a quick glance up at Oaklyn to find her waggling her brows. I stuck out my tongue and brought the phone to my ear. "Hello?"

"Hey." One word and a shiver worked its way down my spine. Heat spread in its wake as I remembered all the ways his words had made me come this weekend. "Just wanted to call and check in. I wanted to make sure you were feeling okay and weren't too sore."

Trying to hide my smile, I dropped my chin and turned away from Aaron. "No, I'm okay," I answered neutrally.

"See, she's smiling," Aaron said victoriously—loudly. "Obviously, she wants me here."

"Who's that?" Kent's voice went from soft and sensual to hard.

"A friend from school." I opened my mouth to explain more, but I didn't need to. Besides, I kind of liked the idea of him being jealous. It was only fair considering the fire that had consumed me when I had known he was with Paige.

There was a long pause, and I held my breath, wondering

what his next words would be. I didn't know him well enough to know how he reacted. Would he hang up? End it here and now? Would he get mad? Not care?

"Will you be home later? I can call you back?"

I expelled the breath I'd been holding. "I should be home later to talk."

"Livvie-baby, you may be home later, but I plan on making you too busy to talk. Your mouth will be busy with other things," Aaron said softly into my hair—just not softly enough to not be heard through the phone.

"Aaron," Oaklyn growled.

I couldn't say anything. The phone almost slipped from my fingers as I turned, slack-jawed, to face him. Burning heat scalded my face, and I wanted to junk-punch him for being such a disgusting, stupid jerk.

"Never mind," Kent's voice pulled me out of my shock. "You're busy. Have a nice night, Olivia."

"Wai—"

But I never got the chance because he hung up before I could explain.

I gently set the phone down on the table, taking deep breaths to regain my composure. But no matter how many deep breaths I took, when I turned to see Aaron's smirking face, only one thought ran through my head.

I was going to fucking kill him.

KENT

THE PLASTIC of the phone dug into my palm, and I waited for the sound of it to crack. I took deep breath after deep breath, but nothing was calming the pulsing beat of jealous rage flooding my veins.

I remembered that voice. It was that little fucking shit from the pizza place. That smarmy fuck that obviously had no respect for Olivia. Yet, she was spending time with him—I checked my watch—at freaking seven in the evening.

"Fuck," I growled, forcing my fists to relax and set down the phone before I crushed it.

I was going to murder that kid. Then I was going tie Olivia to the bed and spank her with my belt before fucking her and reminding her who she belonged to. My cock hardened, completely blotting out any voice trying to remind me she didn't belong to me.

Instead, I clung to the image I'd created and let the pleasure of taking control wash away the tension cramping my muscles.

The door to my hotel room opened, and I turned my back to hide my arousal. But seeing Daniel stroll in, had my erection completely fading and the tension roaring back. Because I was fucking his niece. I had done filthy, dirty things to the girl he looked at like a daughter of his own, and I was a horrible friend because of it.

"What's wrong with you?" he asked.

I struggled to relax my clenched jaw and fists. Rolling my shoulders back, I went for my usual aloof tone. "Nothing."

It didn't work. If anything, his brows furrowed harder. He scrutinized me like a bug under a magnifying glass. His stare was like the sun beating down and making me sweat.

"Did something go wrong with the hotel?" he asked slowly. Daniel knew me better than anyone, and he knew when something was wrong, but it wasn't like I could come out and tell him I was jealous of his niece fucking someone else when I'd just got done defiling her this weekend.

And just like that, my anger was back.

Olivia and that limp-dick kid weren't here to take my anger out on. But Daniel was. "I said nothing. Jesus, can't I just not be happy-go-fucking-lucky all the damn time."

Daniel threw his hands up in surrender. "Someone's edgy."

"I'm fine," I ground out.

He walked further into the room, patting my shoulder on his way to the minibar. "Well, I know how to make you more *fine*." He passed me a glass and leaned against the bar. "Let's hit up that club I told you about. You can take your frustrations out on some willing woman. I know how rough you like it."

Yeah, he did. Which was why he would flip if he knew I'd slept with Olivia. Because it wasn't just knowing I'd slept with her, Daniel would know what I'd done to her—how rough I'd been with the sweet princess of the family.

I scoffed into my drink. *Sweet?* Hardly.

"My contact told me about some of their new equipment we can check out and possibly use for a room at Voyeur." He took a sip of his drink and cocked his brow. A sure sign Daniel had a devious plan. "It's been a while since we've been to a BDSM club. Maybe we can find a woman we both like."

It wasn't uncommon for us to share a woman. We'd done it since we first met in college. But the thought of touching someone else other than Olivia had my stomach churning and a resounding no pulsing through me. Trying to be casual, I gave a shrug. "No, I'm good."

"You're good?" he asked slowly, his brows rising into his hairline.

"Yeah, I'm just not up for it."

"What?"

Daniel stared at me like I'd lost my mind. And why wouldn't he? When did Alexander Kent ever turn down a good time? Damn near never, and we both knew it. I stared down at the amber liquid I swirled in the glass. Anything to avoid Daniel's assessing stare.

"Holy. Shit."

"What?" I asked, still not looking up.

"You're seeing someone." That had my gaze snapping up to his. His blue eyes sparked with victory. "The great Kent—biggest womanizer of them all—plays the field so he can have all the pussy—is seeing someone and only wants her."

Each description he used of me grated on my nerves. "I'm not seeing anyone," I grumbled.

"Oh, bullshit," he called me out with ease. "Her pussy must be golden."

"Jesus." I downed the contents of my glass, trying not to think too hard about how Daniel was calling his niece's pussy golden.

"Hey, maybe if she likes me too, I could join you one night to find out how golden her pussy is. I know you like them kinky."

I slammed the empty glass down on the table. "I said I'm not seeing anyone," I shouted.

Any teasing left Daniel's face, and he wasn't assessing anymore; he was back-tracking because rarely had I ever lost my temper on my best friend. "Okay, dude. Calm down."

I turned away and ran a hand through my hair. I needed to get it together, but it was hard because he was too close to the truth. And just the mention of sharing Olivia with anyone caused a fire to roar through me. It should have been the loudest warning. I loved sharing women with Daniel. I loved sharing women. Period.

But there was no way in hell, I ever wanted anyone to touch what was mine.

Blaring alarm bells rang through my head, and I fought to swallow down the panic.

I was beginning to care about her, and the realization had a rock sinking in my stomach because it was Daniel's fucking niece

—his family. But my body rejected the mere thought of staying away. It also rejected the thought of explaining to Daniel that I had feelings for his niece. We'd come to blows only once over a woman before, and it had ended in a pact of bros before hoes. But we'd been young and determined to not let anything get between us again.

We were almost forty now. Surely, he'd understand if I was serious enough—if he knew that this no longer felt like a fling.

He *would* understand. I knew my friend enough to know that eventually, he'd understand. I just needed to be sure that it *was* more than a fling. Olivia was spending the night with another guy, and here I was having an internal panic over feelings, lashing out at my friend.

"We'll just grab some dinner and some drinks. Talk shop," Daniel said softly behind me. It was enough for me to portray a calm, I didn't quite feel, and face him.

"Yeah, that sounds good. I guess I'm just stressed from the hotels and possibly opening another Voyeur."

"It's a lot, man. But I'm here for whatever you need."

He always had been, and I couldn't imagine losing that. Maybe a couple drinks were just what I needed to calm down and take my mind off Olivia.

Daniel was collecting his keys and heading to the door when I shot off one last text message. I needed to remind her whose dick made her come harder than any little boy.

Kent: Thursday night at 7pm. Room 1469.
Kent: Follow direction.

16 OLIVIA

My phone vibrated on the table, halting Oaklyn's pen across the paper. My heart thumped hard like it had any time Kent's name displayed on my screen in the last month. It'd been two weeks since he'd *punished* me for the whole Aaron debacle. He punished me so well, I almost wanted to try and make him mad again.

"Are you going?" she asked.

She knew I would. She just liked making me admit it. She liked making me face that I jumped whenever he called. I tried to be aloof, but her condescending smile called me out. Oaklyn spent the last couple weeks looking like she was a second away from patting me on the head and telling me my denial was cute.

"You know I am."

"And why is that?" she asked, playing dumb.

"Probably something to do with the five orgasms a night he gives me."

"Uh-huh. And nothing to do with the way you giggle when he calls or how happy you look the next day."

"Of course I'm happy. Hello? Good sex."

"I know a good sex smile, and then, I know a I'm falling for you smile. You definitely have the latter."

"I do not. How can I fall for him if I barely know him?"

"That's a good point." She shrugged and went back to taking notes.

I opened Kent's message and responded, letting him know I'd be there soon.

"Oh, hey, before you go, what was the name of that wine you were talking about the other week."

"It's a Tempranillo. It's Kent's favorite. He said it paired perfectly with steak. I swear he could eat steak every night. That and fettuccini alfredo."

"That's right. It was the same night you wore that sexy red lingerie we bought last year."

"Blue."

"Blue? I thought it was red?"

"It was, but I ordered another set because blue is Kent's favorite color, and I wanted to surprise him."

"Hmm," Oaklyn leaned back, giving me a narrow-eyed stare, nodding slowly.

"What?"

"So, you don't know him, but you know his favorite foods and drinks, and favorite color. And all of that was barely prompted. I could only imagine what else you have tucked away."

"I also know what he tastes like. How he sounds when he comes and his favorite position. On top, because he likes that he can see every part of my body."

"TMI, Olivia."

"But that doesn't mean, I'm falling for him. So what, that I know some of his favorite things. It's all superficial. It's not like I know about his family, or his traditions, or his past."

"But you want to."

"I—" I stuttered and had to swallow before I could get the denial out. "I do not."

"Okay."

Glaring, I shoved my books in my bag and didn't justify her condescending okay with a response.

"Just admit it," Oaklyn pushed.

"There's nothing to admit."

"Olivia—"

"I'll see you tomorrow."

I needed to get out of that room. Oaklyn put me under a microscope, and I didn't want to look that closely at myself. Superficial was safe. And she was wrong. I didn't want to know if he was a mama's boy. Or if he had any nieces and nephews. I didn't want to know what he did for the holidays, so I could imagine me by his side.

I didn't want any of that.

Repeating the words over and over again on the cab ride over, I tried to reclaim the excitement I had when I first saw his name flash on my screen, but Oaklyn's words were like an annoying buzz, I couldn't ignore no matter how hard I tried. By the time I made it to the hotel, I had it mostly under control.

At least, I thought I did until I stepped inside to find Kent's hands clasped on a beautiful gazelle of a woman's shoulders, smiling down at her with familiar affection. I almost choked in shock when she pressed a soft kiss to his cheek, and he. Freaking. Let. Her.

I schooled my features into a blank mask, prepared to give nothing away if he looked over.

My expression may have been placid, but inside was chaos and turmoil.

I don't care.

I don't care if he's with someone else.

All I care about is what he does to me in that room.

It's sex. Just like with Aaron.

I don't care.

But those thoughts were in a losing battle of wanting to know everything. It was like watching him with that woman shined a light on the box I shoved all my feelings in. I always knew it was there, but I put every ounce of fear of being hurt on top of it and denied, denied, denied. But each knowing smile from Oaklyn over the past week chipped away at the lock I kept it all under, and things were spilling out.

Questions I never thought I'd want to ask were bubbling to the surface.

I wanted to demand who the hell that was. I wanted to demand that he never touch another woman besides me. I wanted to demand he was mine always—that I was his. I wanted to demand it all.

Oaklyn's words wreaked more havoc than ever as I tried to portray calm and cool. I walked right past Kent, not acknowledging him on my way to the elevator. I couldn't face him right then. I needed a moment's reprieve to collect my thoughts before he came up.

A hand snuck through the closing doors that slid open to reveal a smiling Kent. I didn't return the smile.

"Hello, Olivia." His voice was like smooth honey sliding over my skin, but I refused to reciprocate. I couldn't—my mind wouldn't allow it.

"Mr. Kent."

I watched him reach for me out of the corner of my eye, but I jerked back before he could make contact.

"Who was that?"

He retracted and stuffed his hand in his pockets, facing the door. "A lawyer."

"You're awfully affectionate with your lawyer."

"Olivia." He sighed like he was tired of dealing with a whiney child.

I wasn't being some petulant baby. This man had me every way he could, and I let him. I had every right to my questions. "Are we exclusive, or are you fucking other women?" I asked. My words snapped in the small space, along with any composure I pretended to have. And out came all the questions and desire to know him more from the box I'd refused to look at. "Hell, where do you even live? Do you have a family? Siblings?"

"I stay with my parents or here when I'm in the city." For every bit of shrill, my voice was, his was equally calm, only spiking my irritation.

I threw my hands out and slapped my thighs when they fell. "See, I didn't even know you had parents."

"Everyone does."

"But are you close? Do you hate them? I know nothing about your past, who you're screwing. *If* you're screwing others—nothing. For all I know, that could have been your wife. I don't even know if you've ever been married."

"I have been," he said, calm like a placid lake. Like he hadn't just dropped a bomb in the tiny elevator.

"What?!" I screeched as the elevator doors slid open.

He finally looked to me with a clenched jaw before grabbing my arm and dragging me to the room.

"When did you divorce? Do you still love her? Does she know about me? Are you still fucking her?" I pelted his back with questions.

When the door to the room opened, he jerked me inside and ground out, "I'm not fucking anyone but you."

"Ugh." I turned my back on him, storming further into the room. I almost laughed at the manic flood of need washing over me. Each wave hit me in the face, washing away any lie I had of wanting Kent to be just a fuck-toy like any other guy I'd known in college. Each wave grew bigger than the last, not letting me hold on to a single ounce of denial. I was raw and vulnerable, and it terrified me. "The thought of you with anyone makes me want to vomit."

Apparently, privacy was all he'd been waiting for because the calm, cool man who'd stood in the elevator exploded. "And you think the thought of you sucking that pencil-dick's cock fills me with fucking joy? Huh?" I turned, unprepared for the torrent of shouts, flushed face, and clenched fists. "I'm not fucking anyone, Olivia, because I can't stomach the idea of being with anyone else. I can't stomach *you* being with someone else. So, whether it's been talked about or not, I'm exclusive to you."

His rant stole all the wind from my sails. "Oh."

"Yeah. Fucking, oh."

I swallowed, trying to find what to say next. He'd calmed the storm, but I still stood there with no armor for whatever came next. Clasping my hands, I tried to calm the tremble spreading through my body. What did I do now? Had I ever been in a position like this? All at once, I felt very immature and without knowledge. I'd never had anything like this with Aaron, and he's the last guy I'd opened myself up to. What was I supposed to say?

"I'm not messing around with him," I said, settling on the most honest thing I could admit in that moment.

"Good."

"I just..." The words bubbled inside me, and I didn't know how to express them—the real reason behind my outburst. I think I surprised us both when I opened my mouth, and a truth I wasn't sure I was ready to share came out. "Ugh! I just care about you, and I don't care if that makes me sound immature and naive. I just hate that I know nothing about you."

Oaklyn would be gloating right about now, letting me know she told me so.

He took a deep breath and kept his eyes on me, the dark

chocolate depths holding a gold mine of answers I wanted to scavenge through. "What do you want to know?" he finally asked softly.

Everything.

I settled on, "You were married?"

His hand dove through his hair, and he expelled a small laugh. "For a little while. Less than a year. We were young and didn't realize our differences until it was too late. We married our senior year, and she thought I would be more serious after graduation. She assumed a lot. She pushed me to be someone I wasn't." He looked away, and by the muscle ticking in his jaw, I assumed it wasn't an easy break. "She almost came between Daniel and me, and I promised to never let anyone control me like that again."

"I'm sorry."

"Don't be. There wasn't enough laughter anyway. I was too young to be so serious at twenty-two."

I scoffed a laugh. "You're not serious now at thirty-eight."

The tension finally eased, only to be replaced with sexual tension when he slowly cocked his brow and tipped his lips. That look had me squeezing my legs. It made promises my body remembered all too well.

"I beg to differ," he said, stalking toward me. "Just because I enjoy the lighter side of life doesn't mean I'm not very serious when it comes to burying my cock in your ass."

He was less than a foot away, and I was ready to let it all go and play. I didn't get many nights with Kent, and I didn't want to spend it arguing. I hadn't sent him running with my confession of caring and freaking out. And somehow, I hadn't sent myself running either. I was ready to let go of the anxiety flooding my veins and have it replaced with something only Kent could give me. I could dig through the now open box tomorrow.

I gripped the sides of my skirt and fisted my hands, tugging the material up higher and higher. "Show me."

His smirk became a full smile. "Gladly."

17 KENT

"So, TELL ME ABOUT YOUR FAMILY," Olivia asked without looking up from her phone.

I'd just stepped out of the bathroom after my shower and stopped dead in my tracks.

She sat with her knees bent and feet off to the side in a pile of fluffy, white down comforter in a white, silk and lace concoction that made up her bra and underwear.

And a large hotel towel wrapped around her head.

It was the epitome of Olivia. Sexy while being unapologetically her. No pretending to be something she wasn't to lure a man in. She laid it all out there, and I loved it.

"Well?"

Pulling my gaze up from her breasts, I found her still holding her phone, but all her attention was on me.

"What was the question?"

Rolling her eyes and groaning, she dropped her phone and moved to the edge of the bed, holding her arms out for me to come closer. I happily obliged, already growing hard when she spread her legs on either side of mine and rested her hands above the towel hanging on my hips. Her thumbs stroked methodically along the ridge of my muscles, looking up at me with innocent eyes, and all I could think was how much I wanted to ruin her in the best way.

"Your family," she said, bringing me out of my fantasy. "Tell me about them. We established you have them, but not much beyond that."

Yeah. Once we began fucking, we hadn't stopped. At least, not to talk. We'd eaten, rested, and woke up to do it all again.

Last night she'd stormed in, a ball of anger and demands. Demands she had a right to know. Demands I wanted to give into. I wanted to share my life with her, and that wasn't a feeling I'd ever had before.

"What do you want to know?"

"Everything."

"I can do that. But first, let's replenish while we talk. I'm not done with you."

I stepped out of her grip and tugged her out into the living room. Junk food, chips, drinks, and board games littered the room from our earlier activities. She'd talked me into a game of Clue and pouted when I kicked her ass, only to turn around and beat me in Ticket to Ride. I'd spanked her as punishment.

I took in her barely covered body when I noticed the bags of food on the table, I'd ordered before my shower. "Did you answer the door like that?"

"Pshh, he wishes. I put on a robe."

"The silk one?"

She shrugged. "Yeah."

"Jesus, Olivia. Let me answer the door from now on."

Her teeth dug into her bottom lip, no doubt holding back her laugh as she stalked toward me. Resting her hands on my waist again, she pushed to her toes and nipped at my chin. "I like you jealous. It turns me on."

Before her hand could undo the knot of my towel, I stepped out of her reach. "Jesus, woman. Give a man some reprieve to recover."

She rolled her eyes and distributed the food.

Perched on a chair, her mouth full of cheeseburger, she went back to her demands. "Talk."

"So, I have a brother, Jacob. He's five years younger and married with a baby."

"What's his wife's name?"

"Lily and their daughter's name is Ava. My parents were high school sweethearts and have been married for forty years. My dad is the CEO of a PR company he started in his basement as a teen. Or that's how he likes to tell it. It was more of an idea in the basement and didn't take off until after college."

"I can see where you get your confidence from," she laughed.

"You could say it runs in the family. Now, my mom. She's the CFO—a fucking genius with numbers."

"It sounds like you have a good relationship with them."

"The best."

"And how is your relationship with your brother?"

"Well, Dr. Phil—"

"Shut up," she said, throwing a fry at me. "Just moving the conversation along."

Laughing, I ate the fry and threw a tater tot back, which she somehow caught in her mouth. Shaking my head, I continued. "Our relationship is okay. Nothing profound, but nothing bad either. I'm closer to Daniel, but I make a point to see Jacob as much as I can. Especially since they had Ava."

"How old is she?"

"Almost one." Snagging my phone from the table, I brought up a picture of Ava smiling to the camera.

"Oh, my gosh. She's adorable."

"And she knows it."

"She must take after her uncle, or is your brother as arrogant as you?"

"I'm not arrogant. I'm confident."

She rolled her eyes but laughed. She loved my confidence, and I loved knowing it.

"How often do you get to see them?"

"Mom is pretty big on doing dinners at least once a month but tries to rope us all in for more if she can."

"It sounds very normal."

"Ninety-nine-point-nine percent. It was nice." My family was a lot like hers in a way, but I didn't need to ask many ques-tions about her life because I knew almost all of it anyway.

"Did they like your wife?"

A bark of laughter broke free. "No, not really. They knew she wasn't right for me but never said anything until after the divorce. They're big on letting us make our own mistakes."

"You mentioned that she almost came between you and Daniel..."

"Yeah," he breathed. "Honestly, I look back, and I'm not even sure how our relationship got started when I remember all the differences between us. Maybe because partying was the priority in all our lives in college. I asked her to marry me, and we did it the next week. Three months later, we graduated, and she went to law school. While I stayed the same, she became more and more reserved."

I looked up, my mouth twisted to the side.

"What?"

"Are you sure you want to hear all this? Some of it includes Daniel."

"You mean Daniel isn't a virgin?" Olivia mock gasped.

"Hardly," I laughed.

"Yes, I want to know. I asked, didn't I?"

"Okay...Well, Daniel and I shared women in college, and on more than one drunken night, we shared Ivette. That was before we got married. On a desperate attempt to pull her out of her reserve, I set up a night with Daniel." I dragged a hand down my face and huffed a laugh. "It didn't go well. At the time, Daniel and I were in the beginning stages of Voyeur—just ideas. She said it was polluting my mind—that *he* was polluting my mind.

"After that night, she refused to have Daniel over. When we were around her law school friends, she'd ask me to lie about Voyeur—about what I was doing. She was embarrassed. It was only the beginning of the lies she asked me to tell, wanting me to hide parts of myself like she was ashamed of me."

"Oh, my god, Kent. She sounds like a raging bitch."

"I think Daniel used those same words."

"I learned how to insult from the best."

"The final straw was when she said she was tired of having to split my time with Daniel. She wanted me to walk away from him and Voyeur. Be respectable were the words she used. Needless to say, I walked away from her. All her demands had added stress to my friendship with Daniel, and in the end, the thought of losing her affected me less than losing my best friend."

"Well, I like who you are."

"Good. Because at this age, I'm not changing."

"Have you been serious with anyone since?" The question was light, but her eyes dropped to her empty box of fries, purposefully avoiding my stare.

"No."

I held my breath, my skin growing taught with each inch she covered scanning up to reach my face. This conversation was toeing the line of dangerous, and I worried my mouth would land us on a bomb waiting to go off.

"Do you want to be?"

Swallowing hard, I considered my answer carefully—not ready to admit too much, but also not wanting to be too flippant and hurt her feelings. "I don't know." I settled with a neutral—if maybe a little cowardly—answer. "I haven't excluded it, but I'm getting older."

Her teeth sunk into her lip, and time slowed, the thudding of my heart ticking away the seconds. After last night, we seemed balanced on the edge of a precipice, and I didn't know which way we would fall. I didn't know which way either of us wanted it to fall, but I think we both knew which way was pulling us harder.

The doubt left me having no idea what her response would be. Would she push for more? Would she be okay with my answer? Would she be hurt by it? I braced myself for impact, unsure of which way the storm would turn.

But nothing ever came. She released the tight grip she had on her lip and smiled the coy smile I knew so well. "You're soooo old."

It took me a moment to catch up on her change of mood. I hadn't been prepared for her to be aloof and let the topic go completely.

Apparently, Olivia—like me—wanted to avoid that conversation. Maybe she saw the hesitation written all over my face and decided to give me a break. No matter what her reasoning was for offering an exit, I was taking it. We could resume this conversation another day.

I lunged across the couch and tackled her, loving her laugh, loving the way it stroked across my skin, bringing it to life. Everything about Olivia brought me to life.

"This old man is about to beat you in strip poker," I declared. We'd had fun playing games all day, and playing one where it got us both naked was everything I needed.

"I need more clothes," she protested.

"I only have a watch and a towel. It's a fair match."

"Fine."

Three rounds later, I was only in my towel and she in her underwear. She lost her towel first and then her bra, and now her damp hair hung past her shoulders, playing peek-a-boo with her nipples. I wasn't even sure what I had in my hand, all my attention focused on just a glimpse of her creamy breasts.

I needed this game over with. Now.

I swapped out two cards and held back my victorious smile. Skin prickling with the end in sight, I prepared my plan for when she finally lost those panties.

"Lay 'em out. Let's see it."

When she still didn't, I pried my stare away from her breasts to find her blue eyes locked on mine. The blue swirled with a dark mix of serious and a hint of light laughter.

"Can I say I don't want you to go?"

It took me a moment to process her question. Apparently, while I'd been lost in coming up with all the dirty things I was going to do to her, she'd gone somewhere else—somewhere more serious. She phrased the question so lightly, but I could hear the nerves shaking her voice. I knew Olivia censored her words with me. I knew there was a whole new depth of meaning and feeling behind her aloof answers, but I always let it slide. If she wanted to talk about something, she knew she could.

But I saw what the question cost her—what it revealed. She wanted to let me know she would miss me but didn't want to give in to make herself vulnerable with a direct confession.

Giving her the same reprieve she gave me earlier, I kept my response light and playful.

"Of course, you can. It inflates my old man ego."

"Shut up," she laughed, throwing her cards down. A pair of twos and two kings.

Only gloating a little, I laid down my four aces. The air thickened with what was to come, a slight flush of her cheeks, her nipples pebbling between the strands of her hair.

"Come here."

When she finally stood before me, I gripped her hips and held her stare, deciding to make myself vulnerable enough for the both of us, "I'll miss you too, Olivia."

18 KENT

THE WORDS on the screen blurred together. I'd been staring at the damn inspection report for hours, and it wore on me. It probably didn't help that I was running on an hour of sleep. I'd caught the red-eye from New York so I could be here for the inspection.

Vivian was supposed to do it, but her husband had a heart attack scare yesterday, and there was no way in hell I'd ask her to leave his side.

The silver lining in the whole mess: Olivia. I could at least take my time here to see her—to feel her in my arms. Half the reason going through this report was taking so long was because I kept getting distracted looking up at every person walking through the door. She should be arriving at any moment, and I had the perfect view from one of the offices.

Every molecule in my body was on high alert to get to her and to lose myself in her. I was exhausted, and the thought of her eased some of the never-ending pressure from the week.

My phone ringing pulled my eyes from the door.

"Kent," I answered.

"Hey, man," Daniel greeted. "How's New York?"

"It was cold, but I'm actually back in Cincinnati. Had a last-minute change and needed to be here for the inspection."

"Shit. That sucks."

I breathed a laugh, pressing my fingers into my eyes to ease the headache brewing. "That about sums it up."

"Did you get a chance to visit the possible site of the new club? I thought it could really work with the location and size. It's two stories which opens up a lot of layout opportunities."

Daniel managed the club and bar—the day to day tasks, while I focused on acquisitions. I'd never had a problem with the roles we fell into. But last night, when I got the phone call saying I needed to fly back, I felt every one of my thirty-eight years, the exhaustion settling heavy into my bones.

I'd craved Olivia more than I'd ever craved anyone, I'd wanted to call her at midnight on my way to the airport just to share the shit that was going on—let her be there with me just so I wasn't so alone in the stress of the day.

And in that moment, I'd envied Daniel and his role that kept him in one place.

"I didn't yet. But when I go back, I'll set up a meeting."

"You sound old, Kent. I mean tired," he joked.

"Ha. Ha. Fuck you."

"Why don't you come by Voyeur tonight? We can have a drink and relax. Sara's been asking about you."

"I can't tonight. I've already made plans."

"Ohh," he said like he knew it all. "With the mystery woman who's been stealing all your extra time."

Just then, a flash of blonde hair caught my eye, and I looked toward the lobby to find a smiling ray of sunshine strutting her way to the elevator. I gripped the chair, fighting the urge to hang up on Daniel and run to her, to take her into my arms and not let go until I could breathe again.

"I care about you."

When she spoke those words last week, they'd rocked me like an earthquake, shaking something loose—creating a crevasse that exposed something I hadn't known existed. I'd almost fallen at her feet and confessed how much I cared for her too, but that had shaken me in its own way. Being with her had started as an ache —a desire and inability to say no to something so tempting, but now it was consuming me.

"I told you, there's no woman. I've just been busy."

"Yeah. Okay," he mocked before continuing like my denial didn't even exist. "Why don't you bring her by," Daniel suggested. "Let me check out this golden pussy and see if I can lure her away from you."

His words were nothing new. It was how we talked to each other all the time. We shared and taunted and flirted with each other's women. Hell, Daniel had even fucked my wife while I watched, and I'd never cared. But with Olivia, something primal beat inside me, bringing out the possessive caveman that had me snapping at my best friend.

"We're almost forty, Daniel. Do you think we can just keep fucking women together? We have to grow up at some point."

"You keep denying it and acting like she's some secret. You never keep secrets from me." His tone was no longer the playful Daniel I knew so well. "So, what the hell is going on?"

"Well, it doesn't mean I can't keep some parts of my life for me. Jesus. I don't have to tell you every damn thing like we're a bunch of teenage girls."

I wished he would have kept arguing back with me. Taken me down a peg. Called me a selfish, pissy asshole.

But he didn't.

He stopped altogether—shut down—and each second that stretched on, my guilt grew. I never snapped at Daniel. We bickered and even brawled, but now, my words were to push him away and make him stop looking where I didn't want him to see.

He was right, I didn't keep secrets, and I knew he felt the wall I was erecting between us. Daniel was more than my friend—he was my brother, and I was pushing him away.

"Listen, I'm just fucking tired and snappy. The two hotels and new club expansion are wearing on me." More silence and I rushed to fill it, to ease the gap widening at an alarming rate. "I'm stressed, and I'm taking it out on you. Probably because I know you're the only one who can handle my pissy-ass mood. Lucky you."

He laughed, but it was forced.

I'd take it.

"Yeah, man. Sorry to push. You're my brother, and I know no one else will take care of your old ass."

I forced my own laugh like a band-aid on a stab wound. "Thanks, D. I'll call you tomorrow, and we can meet up with Carina about the club in New York."

I hung up the phone and slouched back in my chair. "Fuck." I only took a moment to collect myself, rubbing at my pounding temples before shaking off the shit phone call.

Olivia was waiting, and I hustled to get to her.

I stood outside the room and took one last breath before swiping the card and opening the door.

As soon as I stepped through and let the door close behind me, a beautiful ball of sex and sin barreled toward me. She leaped in my arms and wrapped around me like a barracuda I never wanted to disentangle from. She peppered kisses all over my face, and before I knew it, I was laughing.

With her in my arms, all was right in my world.

19 OLIVIA

I COULD'VE SPENT every morning for the rest of my life this way, curled up in Kent's arms. My ear pressed to his chest, listening to the thud of his heart as my hand played in the ridges and valleys of his abdomen. I almost purred from the way he pet my hair between fisting the locks and tugging them just because he could, and he liked the way my skin broke out in chills from the light sting.

That thought should have terrified me. A couple weeks ago, it would have. Now, it still created anxiety pressing on my chest, but it was more a cat than an elephant. The fear of being vulnerable was there, but it wasn't as scary anymore. It was like Kent turned the lights on and showed me the boogieman wasn't so bad.

Didn't mean the boogieman didn't exist. I was just able to look him in the eye and tell him to fuck off.

"I have to leave again this evening. My business wasn't done in New York," his voice vibrated against my cheek, and I tried not to tense at the news.

His message to meet him last night was unexpected, but I hadn't cared, I was grateful to get more of him.

My first instinct was to pout and demand more of his time, demand we stay locked in this hotel room until we were old and gray.

Instead, I settled for a simple, "Okay."

It wasn't anything new from the last month, but it didn't make it any easier. It'd been a week since our argument. A week since I opened Pandora's box and admitted that I did really care.

If I thought I cared about this man before, nothing compared to now. I discovered the hard-working man beneath the light-hearted veneer, the caring man, the loving son, brother, and uncle. When he sent me a picture of him with his niece, my heart almost combusted along with my ovaries.

Everything was still the same, but also very different. We still only met at the hotel for quick romps, but sometimes it was more than that. Sometimes, I brought my comfy jammies and curled into his chest, watching movies and eating popcorn. Our phone calls were more about getting to know each other, rather than sexually taunting each other.

It'd only been a few days, but when I thought about it, we'd been shifting for a while. It was just this last week, we embraced it. And I loved everything about it. I never wanted anything to change. I wanted to live in this man's arms in this hotel room, forever.

But forever came to a screeching halt when his hand stopped moving in my hair and rumbled the words, "I think we should tell Daniel."

Everything stopped. My heart, my thoughts, my breathing, *his* breathing.

"What?" I whispered.

"Olivia..."

I jerked to my elbow, needed to see if he was really serious. "Why? Why would you want to tell him?"

His brow furrowed. "I don't know, Olivia. Maybe because I care about you and want more than this room with you?"

"I do too, but that doesn't mean we have to tell Daniel."

"It doesn't? What about when I want you by my side at social events? Or I want to hold your hand at dinner? What then?"

My heart pounded, thrumming like a freight train, bringing every inch of my skin alive. My lungs worked double-time to compensate for the extra blood pumping in my veins. "I—I don't know."

I closed my eyes and imagined telling Daniel I was screwing his best friend. I imagined his eyes dimming, the pride slipping away as he saw me the same way as everyone else—a girl only good for her body. What if he thought I slept with Kent to get the internship? What if he thought all the good things everyone said about me at the hotel were all because I was screwing the boss.

"Olivia..."

"What do you want me to say to him, Kent?" Pulling the sheet to my chest, I moved from the haven of his arms, needing space. "Hey, Uncle Daniel. The internship is going great. Mainly because I'm screwing the boss. Life is pretty easy when you don't have to use your brain and just your body."

"That has nothing to do with us, and you know it," he growled, his own frustration rising now.

"And he'll know exactly what I let you do to me. How could he not? He's been your fuck partner for as long as I've been alive. He'll know everything."

"Olivia—"

"God, the way he'll look at me. I—I'll be a disappointment."

"You're being dramatic."

"I get to be dramatic," I screeched. "I'm just a silly girl who gets to be dramatic."

"Stop," he barked. "That's enough."

But I was beyond his commands. This wasn't sex, and he

didn't get to boss me around outside of bed. "He's like my father, and you're asking me to tell him I have dirty hotel sex with his best friend. I mean, what happens if it doesn't work out? Who will he choose? Will I be the cause of your friendship ending?"

I dropped the sheet and searched for my dress. Snatching it off the floor, I struggled to untangle the material with my shaky hands, and tears blurring my eyes. This was everything I was scared of, finally admitting I cared and something going wrong and having to endure the crumble.

"Olivia," he said, but I ignored him. I didn't know what else to say. I was in a tailspin of panic and needed to get out of there. "Olivia," he said again, this time tinged with his own panic now that I had my dress on. "What are you doing?"

I stopped. What was I doing? Running from the moment? Running from the man? I looked at him sitting up in bed and really saw him. I locked my eyes on his, and it was like I could breathe again. Inhaling as deep as my lungs would allow, I calmed down. The panic was still there, simmering, but I didn't want to run from Kent. I didn't want to give up at the first bump in the road.

"I'm scared," I admitted on a whisper.

"I understand. But I also know Daniel."

"You know Daniel as your best friend. The guy who cheers on your conquests."

Kent laughed. "Trust me, Daniel won't be cheering me on when it comes to you. But he also won't overreact. I know him, Olivia."

I did too. I knew he was the only person to ever expect more of me. More than stumbling into a sex club and sleeping with the first man I met. What if he found out, and that was how he saw me? Who would expect more of me then?

"Olivia, please."

Time stood still, and I remained frozen to the spot. "Why?" I finally whispered.

"Why what?"

"Why would you want to risk it? What if all this blows up in our faces? Why risk it?"

He floundered, his mouth opening and closing, and it was like a pin to my balloon. I deflated. Maybe he did only want me for sex, and he couldn't think of a valid reason to risk it all beyond a good blow job.

"Forget I asked," I said when his answer took too long to come.

"Oli—"

"I have to go."

"Because I love you."

The words ripped from him. They tore from him and slammed into me so hard, I lost my breath.

"What?"

"Okay?" he growled, one hand thrown out and the other buried in his hair. "I love you. It's got about a million strings attached to it that could go wrong, but there it is."

The words rippled across my skin, sinking into my body, filling my chest up like a balloon that was going to float away. Every bit of anxiety over Daniel fled, no room for it among all the joy stretching me from head to toe.

Kent loved me.

Kent loved me.

My mind played the words on repeat until it bubbled over. Abandoning my exit, I jumped on the bed, giggling at his wide eyes. His arms automatically came up to catch me, and I climbed on his lap, wrapping around him, trying to become one with him.

It wasn't enough. His brow furrowed like he wasn't sure what to expect next, and I laughed again. I couldn't blame him. We'd been awake all of an hour, and our emotions had swayed from one extreme to the next like a rollercoaster.

But I'd ride it again and again if it got me in his arms, weightless and happy. Wiping away any doubt, only one truth remained.

"I love you too," I whispered before fusing my lips to his. I put all of myself into it—gave him every part of me. It took less than a second before he gave all of himself in return.

Kent and I had passionate, wild, crazy sex that always took me to the ends of the Earth, but this was more. This was Earth-shattering. This was us clinging tight to put ourselves back together in each other's arms.

"We're so fucked," he grumbled, his lips skimming down my neck, his hands fisting my dress out from between us.

"I don't care." I was a geyser exploding with emotion, and I was unable to hold it in. I laughed and kissed any inch of skin I could reach. "I don't care because I love you."

My core brushed against his hardened shaft, and I shifted until I could slide up and down his cock, coating him with my desire, moaning each time he brushed my clit.

"I need you," he moaned.

"Yes."

Before leaning back to grab a condom, he gripped my jaw and forced me to meet his eyes. "We have to tell him, Olivia. He's my best friend, and I can't keep lying to him. He knows something is going on with me, and it's only adding tension. Give him a chance to understand."

"Just..." I swallowed and flicked my eyes to the side, collecting myself. "Just give me time."

It wasn't perfect. It didn't fix all the things that could go wrong running through my mind, but it was a step in the right direction. I could do this—with him—one step at a time.

How could I not when I loved him?

20 KENT

I HELD my breath when the door creaked, and a shaft of light spread across the foyer, only to be filled with Olivia's shadow. I waited for her to notice me despite the way I sat in the dark corner of the room, but instead, she let the door slowly close behind her and followed the directions on the paper clutched in her hand.

Only the dim light in the foyer was on, illuminating another note on the table. She unfolded the paper and let out a snort that almost had me laughing. I imagined her doing this before every time we met. Scoffing at my demands but doing them anyway...for me.

My cock grew hard as I watched her strip away her dress and open the box that was under the note. She lifted the lid, and a small gasp reached across the dark room and sank into my skin, reminding me of all the other times she'd made that sound under my ministrations.

She lifted the black silky material and slid the dress on. She looked perfect, just like I imagined. The material draped over her subtle curves perfectly, and I couldn't wait to reveal them again later. I bit back my moan when she did a happy dance, bouncing from one foot to another before pulling out the black, glittering pumps with the red sole. Olivia loved fancy things, and tonight, I planned on giving them all to her.

She slid the shoes on—making even that simple movement unbearably sexy—and faced the dark hotel room as she'd been instructed.

She was so perfect I could've spent the entire night just watching her stand there like a regal queen waiting to be ravaged. But my cock had other plans.

Her eyes snapped to mine when I flicked the light on. I could've died right then with the way her lips spread in the most beautiful smile I'd ever seen. All because I was here. It did things to my ego. It did things to the organ thumping harder in my chest.

God, I loved this woman. I wasn't sure what I was going to do about it, but I knew I loved her, and that had to be enough for now.

"Kent," she breathed.

"Hey, beautiful." She was so bold, but the blush that stained her cheeks at my simple compliment belied her youth and innocence. "I wanted to create a date just for us," I explained, gesturing to the white cloth-covered table.

I wanted to take her out on the town, show her off, but she'd made herself clear that she needed time. It wasn't what I wanted, but I respected her enough to be understanding of her decision.

For now.

"Come here," I ordered.

She obeyed, as always.

I hit the button for the stereo, turning on bluesy jazz, and stood to greet her. When she stood only a foot away, her chin tipped up just enough to look me in the eyes, I dug out the slim platinum chain from my pocket, dangling it between us.

"What is that?" she asked breathlessly.

I slid the metal around her neck. "I'm not into the BDSM lifestyle seriously, but I do love the idea of this on you at all times. My way of claiming you—marking you—even when I'm not around."

Moving behind her, I shifted her to stand in front of the mirror. Her fingers grazed the metal, her mouth falling open in a small oh. "It's beautiful. Thank you."

I brushed her hair to the side and placed lingering kisses from her shoulder to her ear, loving the soft exhale as she tipped her head to the side, giving me access to every inch of her.

"Come sit down. Dinner is waiting."

"I thought it smelled good in here."

"I even had it prepared the way you like it, medium-rare." I shuddered at the overdone meat. "So savage."

She sat, rolling her eyes. "It's only one step above what you order."

"Still too much."

"Well, thank you. This all looks delicious."

She moaned when she bit into the first slice of her steak, and I forced myself to do the same instead of forgoing dinner to ravage her on the table. The candlelight flickered over her features, and if I tried hard enough, I could almost imagine us at home having a normal dinner we could enjoy every night. She was radiant, and a part of me, I never knew was there, longed for it to be true.

She sipped from her wine and rested her elbow on the table and her chin on her hand, smiling across the table. "So, how's business?"

"Which business?" I asked with a laugh tinged with the exhaustion that had been riding me for weeks.

"The ones in New York."

I got distracted when her other elbow rested on the table too, and her dress gaped, exposing her cleavage. "Umm...what?"

Her lips tipped up, her smile knowing. "The New York businesses, Kent."

"Right, right. Sorry, your luscious tits distracted me." That earned me another blush. "They're going well. We closed on the hotel building and should be making final decisions on the location of the new club."

"That's so amazing. Daniel manages Voyeur, so who will handle everything in New York?"

"We'll hire someone, and Daniel will run point with him. And I travel to New York enough we can keep a close eye on it all."

"Sounds amazing. Will you do the same design at the club in New York as you have now?"

"Something close."

"Oh," she held up her finger and ran to grab her phone before perching at the edge of the seat next to me. "I was going through Pinterest and saw these club chairs that totally reminded me of the whole gentleman's club you've got going on, already."

She held the phone out for me to look, her face alight with pride at her discovery, and she was stunning. She was so beautiful and smart, and she had no idea what to do with all the genius ideas running through her head. I looked down at the picture of the high-back, dark leather chairs. They were both classically sophisticated, but modern too.

"They're a new, local shop that refurbishes furniture they find at auctions and other places. Kind of like that one show on American History. It's super cool."

"You know," I started, sitting back in my seat. "Carina is starting a new marketing venture with a whole design team. It might be something you'd enjoy."

"Trying to get rid of me, Kent."

"Hardly. I'm a selfish man, and I want to keep you all to myself. But your class will be over soon, and as you progress through your classes, you may need another internship. It will look good on your resume."

"You're probably right."

I rested my hand over hers. "You're so talented, Olivia, and I think you haven't even begun to tap into your potential."

She bit her lip and dropped her gaze to her lap, but not before I saw yet another blush and smile.

"Thank you."

"It's true. Anyone would be lucky to have you on their side. You have brilliant ideas."

She lifted hopeful eyes to mine. "Maybe I can go to New York with you and help her if she's interested."

I perked up at her suggesting plans outside of this hotel suite. "I would love that."

"Does Daniel go with you?"

"Sometimes."

"Oh." The excitement of the moment dimmed, and I hated having this thing lingering between us. We stretched in limbo, unsure of where we would fall next.

"Have you talked to him?"

"Not recently," she answered lightly. Completely opposite of the heavy pressure weighing on my chest. "I was supposed to see him for lunch the other day, but I had to cancel because of homework."

I wanted to believe she wasn't avoiding him, but the way she refused to look up from her plate had doubt seeping in.

I brushed it off, sure it was nothing. Olivia wasn't someone to hide from honesty. She was straightforward, one of the many things I loved about her. "How about dessert?" I asked, eager to leave this topic behind, and enjoy the rest of our date.

Her shoulders dropped, the tension leaving her body, and she finally looked up and smiled. "Sure."

"Wait here," I ordered, standing and grabbing the bowls of

whipped cream and strawberries. With everything I needed in hand, I ordered, "Follow me."

"What?" she asked when I walked past her toward the bedroom.

"Come. Here."

We stood by the closed doors, and I nodded toward the handle, silently requesting she open for me. When she did, her hand flew to her mouth, and she sucked in a breath.

Candles and rose petals touched almost every corner of the room, creating a romantic oasis I couldn't wait to worship Olivia's body under.

"Kent." She turned to me, her eyes damp and sparkling in the flickering candlelight. "It's so beautiful. I don't know what to say."

"Don't say anything. Just take that dress off and lay back on the bed. I'm ready for my dessert."

21 OLIVIA

"Let's go skydiving."

Tipping my head back from its perch on the arm of the couch, I took in Kent dressed in a suit. Even upside down, he looked delicious. He'd stepped out of the hotel room to take a phone call and apparently came back in a madman.

"What?"

"Skydiving."

Like I didn't know what the words meant. "Ummm...no, thanks." I laughed and leaned back up to flip through my magazine. "I'm all for being adventurous, but I prefer to do it with both feet on the ground. Besides, don't you need practice for something like that?"

"Not really," he answered, perching himself on the edge of the couch by my legs. "Not if you're strapped to someone."

"Still a hard pass."

"Okay, then. Let's try something else."

"What is it?"

"A surprise." His eyes promised more than an adventure.

"Tell me."

He pushed my magazine away and leaned over, caging me in with an arm on each side of my head. "Don't you trust me?" His voice was like a rough siren calling me out to play.

"Not if you're going to push me out of a plane."

"Scaredy. Pants." His lips moved slowly, forming each word to enunciate the insult. Each word dropped with its own challenge. He knew how much I couldn't turn down a challenge. He issued them all the time.

I bet you can't come again.

I bet you can't take me fucking your throat.

I bet you can't come just from me playing with your nipples.

My eyes narrowed, and I pushed up on my elbows, forcing him back. "Excuse me?"

"You heard me." He smirked, knowing he had me. "Big. Baby."

"Fine," I growled, shoving him back. "Bring it on, tough guy."

"OH, MY GOD. THAT WAS AMAZING."

I gripped his shoulders, bouncing on the balls of my feet.

He'd taken me indoor skydiving. I'd been hesitant at first, worried I'd end up spiraling out of control and hitting the glass. I'd be on the news later that night. *Girl dies while skydiving in a plastic tube.* But the instructor had carefully explained that he wouldn't let me go, and Kent hadn't dropped that challenging smile until I finally gave in.

"Enough to do the real thing?"

"Fuck no. Floating in a tube of air is a lot different than falling toward imminent death out of a plane."

He threw his head back and laughed, and I fought to not lean in and bite at his neck. My adrenaline was through the roof. The weightless feeling I'd had in the tube followed me out. The adrenaline flooding my veins vibrated under my skin, and I became desperate for an outlet. Not caring of the two instructors standing a few feet away, I gripped Kent's neck and jerked him down to me, attacking his mouth. His body froze for less than a second before he gripped me tight, and it became a battle of wills in the kiss.

We bit, sucked, and moaned like animals.

"I could get used to this wild side of you," he said when he pulled back for air. "Will you go on more adventures with me, sweet Olivia?"

"Anything." I'd do anything if it gave me this high again.

"How do you feel about bungee jumping?"

Except that. The thought alone had my arousal plummeting. I still ached but at manageable levels. "What is with you wanting to take me off solid ground?"

"I have to sweep you off your feet any way I can."

"That was a corny line," I laughed.

"It's my old-man charm."

I nipped his chin, loving the scrape of his scruff against my lips. "I like your old-man charm—and by charm, I mean the way you fuck me." He lunged for me, but I ducked away, laughing.

"Tease," he growled.

"If you feed me, I could be persuaded to give in. All this excitement is burning up my energy, and I need to replenish."

"We can't have that. Let's head back to the hotel then."

"I'm tired of the food there," I whined.

"There's an easy solution for that," he hinted. Not very subtly though. I knew he was suggesting that we go out to eat, and he knew I still hadn't talked to Daniel. "How about this," he started when I remained stubbornly silent. "What if we went to your place and picked up food on the way?"

"Daniel lives in my building."

"I'm aware of that."

"What if we run into him?"

"Well, we could always explain that we're in love and spending time together."

"Kent..."

"Or we could rely on the fact that we probably won't see him, and if we do, I'll tell him I was just making sure you got home after a meeting."

I mulled the idea over, and he watched me carefully like I was a bomb about to go off. He was a man on the edge of his seat, wanting to ask for more but holding back for me. And if he could do that, then I could do this for him.

"Okay. Take me home. But I want Chinese for dinner tonight."

"Yes, ma'am."

We stripped out of our jumpsuits and headed home. Kent kept making my heart leap out of my chest by saying, "Hi, Daniel," once we got into the lobby, even though no one was there.

"You're not funny, you know?" I said around a mouthful of lo mien.

He leaned back against my couch from his position on the floor, crossed legs stretched out in front of him, munching on an egg roll. "I don't know, I make you laugh a lot."

"Total pity laughs."

He threw a piece of broccoli my way, and I expertly caught it in my mouth.

"Nice try."

"Find a new skill of yours every day."

"Well, then tell me a hidden skill of yours. We need to even the score."

"Hmm..." He thought it over as he scooted closer to me. "I'm really good at bowling." Once he was within reach, he nodded toward my container. "Give me some of your lo mien."

I scooped up a bite with my chopsticks and carefully lifted it to his open mouth. "You'll have to take me someday."

"You bowl?"

"I have bowled, but I'm more of a roller-skating rink kind of gal."

"I will happily watch from the side-lines."

"Maybe I'll teach you someday."

"What else does the beautiful and talented Olivia Witt like to do?"

"Hmm..." I thought of what else I loved to do. The first thought was to say something sexy because that was what most guys wanted to hear. But Kent looked at me like he wanted to see below the surface. Like he wanted to know what I really liked to do. The truth bloomed in my chest and radiated out, filling every inch of me to almost bursting. "Do you trust me?" I asked, an idea taking root.

His eyes narrowed, but after only a moment's hesitation, he finally said, "You know I do."

"Okay. Help me clean up, and we can get started."

"With what?"

"It's a surprise," I said with a wink, returning the taunting he'd given me this morning.

Thirty minutes later, we lounged back on the chaise of my couch. Me between his legs with his arms wrapped tight, his heart thudding perfectly behind me.

"I can't believe I'm doing this."

"If I can skydive, then you can do a facial."

"How much longer do we leave this on for? And what is that smell?"

I tipped my head back to look up at his light green face. He kind of did look ridiculous, especially with the scowl. Somehow, he also looked more masculine with his dark scruff defined jaw.

"I love you," I whispered.

His face softened and looked down, pouring all his love and adoration into me. "I love you too." Despite the cream, he hunched over and softly kissed my lips. "But seriously, how long and what is that smell."

Laughing, I resituated myself to watch Tim Gunn look over a half-finished dress. "It's cucumber, and I leave it on for one episode of Project Runway."

"I've smelled cucumber, and this is not it."

"May also be the yogurt."

"Jesus, woman. What do I have on my face?"

"You'll thank me for it later. I promise."

"So, this is what you do while I'm away?"

"Yup. I'm not as glamorous as I seem."

"Nonsense," he said before kissing the top of my head. "Do you want to be a fashion designer? Is that your end goal?"

"I don't know. I don't think so. I just like design in all its forms. Clothes, interior, or art. I like the concept of taking one small bland item and mixing it with another to create something eye-catching."

He paused, trailing his fingers up and down my arms, leaving goosebumps in his wake. "It suits you."

"Daniel said so too. Mom always kind of patted my head and told me my designs were pretty, but Daniel pushed me to do more. He saw more than just a girl who liked clothes."

"It's pretty easy to see if someone takes the time to look at you and really see you."

His words were simple and said without any hesitation, but they sunk in and hit a spot not many people were able to reach— not a spot I *let* many people reach. Fire burned the backs of my eyes, and I blinked to keep the tears at bay.

"Thank you, Alexander."

"Only stating the truth, Olivia."

I hunched over and kissed his arm, just needing to show him

an ounce of affection for the impact of his words. "You should stay tonight," I whispered against his skin.

He stiffened for only a moment. "Are you sure?"

I loved that he asked. I knew how much he wanted me to talk to Daniel. I knew how much it cost him to be around his best friend and not admit what we were doing. But I still couldn't bring myself to say the words just yet, the fear of the unknown, of losing someone who sees me beyond my cute love of clothes, terrified me, and I wasn't ready.

I loved him for understanding, and I wanted him in my bed tonight. I may not be able to admit our truth just yet, but I could give him this. "Yes. Now, quiet, they're about to do the runway show. I also like to critique and see if mine come close to the judges."

"Yes, ma'am. Judge away."

My eyes cracked open and caught on the vision staring back at me. I was lying on my side, facing the mirror with a strong arm tossed over my waist. In my bed. Not a hotel bed with impersonal sheets, but *my bed*, with my familiar teal bedspread and gray pillows.

I loved every moment with Kent, but this had to be one of my favorites. This felt the most real. It was everything I wanted in a single reflection.

The arm around my waist tightened, and warm lips pressed to my neck as his hand shifted to cover my breast.

"Good morning."

My heart tumbled over his gruff morning voice and fell at his feet. I turned to face him and softly kissed his lips. "Good morning. Do you want some coffee?"

"Hell, yes."

"Why don't you stay in bed, and I'll go make us some."

He moved all at once, covering my body with his, sinking me into the mattress. My thighs spread around his hips. He buried his head in my neck, kissing the skin as he thrust, sliding his hard cock along my wet slit.

"As much as I want to stay here all day buried in your tight pussy, I have meetings. So, while you're getting coffee, I'm going to shower."

I gave him my best fake pout, which had him laughing before getting out of bed, standing and stretching in all his naked glory. Kent may have been almost forty, but his body was better than any college boys I'd seen.

The confidence he had strutting around the room, collecting his clothes, his thick length swaying between his firm thighs had me almost begging for him to come back to bed.

"If you keep staring, I'm going to miss my meetings."

"Sorry." But I was anything but sorry, and we both knew it.

When he disappeared behind the door, I considered joining him but didn't want to make him late. I pulled up an app and ordered some breakfast to be delivered and got the coffee started.

I'd just finished pouring our mugs when there was a knock on the door. I made sure my robe was tightened, so I didn't reveal anything scandalous to the delivery guy. Opening the door, my whole world froze. Stopped spinning completely for a solid ten seconds before it very quickly began to spiral into an imminent crash.

"Uncle Daniel." Was that my voice? It sounded like a mouse.

"Hey, kid." He ruffled my hair and stepped past me into the living room. "Sorry to swing by unannounced, I was about to leave when your mom asked me to make sure you come to dinner this week. She let me know her text messages weren't enough to get you over and encouraged a face-to-face so you couldn't say no."

My laugh bubbled out high-pitched and a little manic. "Did she?"

He looked around, and I stepped between him and the two mugs sitting blatantly on the counter. Thankfully, the shower had turned off before I answered the door, and now, I had to hope Kent didn't stroll out, and it ended like a bad cliché.

"Is now a bad time? You don't have a boy over, do you?"

"Oh, my god. No. I would never." Okay, too much of a denial. *Pull it back, Olivia.* Relaxing my shoulders, I went for a nonchalance that felt lightyears away from the panic flooding every inch of me. "I don't have time for silly boys."

"That's my girl." Daniel ruffled my hair like he did when I was a kid. "So, you'll be there?"

"Yeah, yeah. Of course."

"Well, that was easy. Maybe I'll be just as lucky when I get Kent to agree to dinner too."

Another high-pitched laugh slipped out. "I'm sure he'll agree."

"I don't know. He's been evasive lately."

"Really?"

Why couldn't I bring my voice down to a normal octave?

"Yeah. Maybe I'll just call him now while my luck is hot."

No, no, no, no, no. Please, God, no.

I watched in horror as he pulled out his phone. My eyes quickly scanned the room, hoping Kent's phone wasn't sitting anywhere in the open. I prayed to the cell-phone gods that his phone was on vibrate, or dead, or was stolen by a magical ghost. Anything other than ringing loud enough for Daniel to hear.

He brought the phone to his ear, and I held my breath for so long I was sure I was going to pass out. Was it connecting? Was it ringing? Had I just frozen time with my force of will? Everything stretched until I finally heard ringing from Daniel's phone but not an answering ring from anywhere in the apartment.

I damn near collapsed in a heap of relief. All the tension that had been holding me upright and clenched tight washed away, leaving me weak.

"Hey, Kent. It's D. Family dinner tomorrow night. Be there or be square. Julia's orders."

And then he hung up.

"Well, I won't keep you any longer. I'll see you tomorrow?"

"Yup."

"Good girl."

He leaned forward and pressed a kiss to my forehead and walked out. My knees decided to give out at the click of the door, and I sagged to the couch.

"Well, that was fucking close," Kent said, coming from the hallway. He collapsed on the couch next to me and ran a hand over his face. "Thank fuck I heard him before coming out. I had enough time to put my phone on vibrate. Jesus fucking Christ."

"Yeah," was all I could get out.

"I'm not sure dinner tomorrow is such a good idea," he said slowly.

"Why?"

He rolled his head to look my way, his furrowed brow hinting at his frustration. "It's hard enough to lie to Daniel about being with you when I'm not in the same room as you."

Guilt hit, knocking the wind out of me. "I'm sorry. I'm just... I just haven't had time."

"Yeah."

His response sounded just as believable as mine. "Would it help to know I'd like having you there. It's not like we'd have to be strangers."

"I don't know, Olivia."

"Please. It's just dinner. Nothing different than any other meal at my parents."

He slowly lifted a brow, calling me on my bullshit because it was very different. We loved each other, and my fears were standing in the way of it.

A beat of silence ticked by before he finally agreed.

"Okay. But we have to act normal. No flirting."

"No flirting."

I'd do my best.

22 KENT

I'd spent the last twenty-four hours trying to figure out a reasonable excuse to not go to dinner tonight. I'd muttered something about an important meeting to Daniel. He'd leveled a look my way that let me know there was no not going.

So, now I sat in the car next to my best friend, to go have dinner with his niece, who he'd almost caught me fucking yesterday, and her parents.

Fucking awesome.

"I'm glad you decided to put your half-ass attempts to the side and come to dinner."

"It's no hardship. Julia is a damn good cook."

"Yeah. My brother lucked out with that one."

There was a wistful note in his voice, and it made me wonder if Daniel was as happy as he used to be about being single all the time.

"I haven't seen you much, and this may make me sound like a teenage girl..." He glared my way, throwing my words back in my face. "But I miss you, man."

Regret pierced my chest as I remembered my callous words.

I'd been a dick when I'd accused Daniel of that just to avoid getting caught in my lie.

"I'm sorry, man. I shouldn't have said that." I gave a sincere apology but followed up with our usual banter. "I love hearing all your teenage feelings. Makes me feel all warm and gooey."

"Fuck you," Daniel said around a laugh.

We drove a couple more blocks before he spoke again.

"I don't know what I'd do without you. You're my ride-or-die. Been there for me since college. There for every crazy idea. Every crazy-ass adventure."

Daniel had loved and lost once in his life, and he'd claimed that was enough to never want to fall that deeply in love again. When college was over, we'd both thrown ourselves into work, travel, adventures, and as many women as we could. It'd always been him and me.

We weren't the kind of guys to talk about our feelings, and the fact that Daniel did, made me feel like an epic heel that somewhere over the past few months, I made him question my loyalty to him as a friend. Because I *was* loyal to him. It wasn't disloyal to be with Olivia.

It was just disloyal to not talk to him about it. I was an almost forty-year-old man, and I knew better. I knew when to talk things over. I knew Daniel would probably initially explode, but quickly recover because he knew me. He'd be able to see the difference and know I loved Olivia.

But I'd left the ball in Olivia's court. She was young and not as sure of herself, and I promised myself I'd be patient with her. I had to have faith in her that she wouldn't drag this out forever. I had to have faith that she knew enough of my past with Daniel to know lying forever wasn't an option.

We loved each other, and I had faith in that love.

"Don't you feel tired sometimes? Tired of the one-night

stands? Tired of constantly moving?" I eased into the topic, trying to get a feel for where he was at. He sounded more somber tonight. Maybe if I could come to Olivia with proof he wouldn't blow up and abandon her like she thought, it'd help her take the next step.

"Says the manwhore who doesn't have a solid home."

I winced, mainly because his words were true. Or they used to be true. Not since Olivia though. "I was actually thinking of buying a place."

He looked over, the lights from the dash illuminating his raised brows. "Oh, yeah? Where?"

"Your building is nice."

"It sure is." His smile grew as though the idea of living in the same building got better and better. "That would be great too because we could double up our security on Olivia. I swear she had a guy in her apartment this weekend."

The smooth conversation I'd envisioned skipped a beat. "Huh." It was the only word I could summon, and I barely breathed it.

I expected him to make the connection any moment, and the ruse would be over. I held my breath the rest of the short drive and was about to scramble out once we pulled into the drive, but he stopped me.

"Listen, Kent." I turned back and watched my friend grip the wheel, keeping his gaze locked on the house. "You know how I feel about relationships. I can't go through it again."

"That was a long time ago."

"It leaves a permanent mark that no time can take away. That's why I'm so grateful for you. If that need hits me and I'm feeling lonely, I hit you up. David is my brother by blood, but you're so much more, and I appreciate you always being there and sticking it out with me."

He lifted his fist and waited. Hating myself for not being able to be one-hundred-percent honest with him, I lifted my hand and bumped his knuckles.

We walked inside and were greeted the way we always were with hugs and kisses. Thank God, Olivia stayed back and only gave a small wave. Even if that wave did come with a sultry stare.

"Hi, Mr. Kent," she'd said.

"Olivia," I barely managed. She flounced into the dining room, her schoolgirl plaid skirt way too short to meet any dress code. My eyes clenched tight to avoid watching, hoping for a glimpse of what lay underneath. I had no idea how I was going to make it through this.

Daniel slapped my back, reminding me of everyone around. "Come on. Let's eat."

Dinner was, as always, delicious. And thankfully, almost over. My body ached from the tension pulling every muscle tight, ready to snap.

She'd tortured me through the meal. Watching me as much as she could, making promises with her eyes, there was no hope of fulfilling tonight. Licking her lips, nibbling them. Arching her back, letting me know she wasn't wearing a bra underneath her thin T-shirt. Each one tightened the screw.

When she stood to collect the plates with her mother, her skirt floated dangerously around her thighs. I was surprised I didn't have a raging headache for how much effort it took to keep my eyes from staying glued to her.

"Drinks in the den?" David asked.

I almost bolted from the room to remove myself from temptation. She was Eve with an apple, and I was a weak, weak man on the edge of giving in.

"Sounds perfect," Daniel answered.

"Ladies, are you joining us?" David asked.

Please no. Please no. Please no.

"A nightcap sounds nice," Julia said.

I held my breath, waiting for Olivia's answer, too scared to look over to let her see the plea in my eyes. I wasn't sure if the plea was to stay away or to pull me closer.

"I think I'm going to head to bed. It's been a long weekend."

Somehow, I managed to remain upright and not slide out of my chair in relief. Thank you, God.

We all went our separate ways, but before heading up the stairs, she looked back over her shoulder and winked. I was so paranoid someone else saw that I didn't take it for the warning it was.

So, almost an hour later, when I stepped out of the bathroom, I should have been prepared for her grabbing my arm and dragging me up the stairs and down the hall.

"Olivia," I whispered, looking behind me, terrified someone was going to come out and see us.

She jerked me into a room and closed the door. Only the soft light of the lamp illuminated the room. Enough for me to see the pink bedspread with a slew of stuffed animals up against the pillows. Enough for me to see the pictures of Olivia at prom or in her cheerleading uniform. Fuck me, I'd have to have her dig that out at some point. I was jerked from my perusal when Olivia whipped her shirt off.

"Olivia!"

I almost laughed at the way I gasped her name like a woman protecting her virtue. Clearing my throat, I tried to keep my eyes on hers as she backed up to sit on the bed. Even if I wasn't directly looking, the sway of her breasts had me growing harder by the second.

"I'm not fucking you here. Your parents are downstairs and will come looking."

"Just a quick BJ, then."

Thighs clenched, I remained rooted to the spot, my hands fisting in my pockets to keep from grabbing her, shoving her to the floor, and fucking her mouth until I came. "I don't think that's a good idea."

She turned sideways on her bed and fell back, letting her head hang off the edge, all that golden hair cascading like an alluring waterfall. "Come on, Kent," she said, dragging her hands up her thighs, pulling her skirt along with it. "You always said you wanted to fuck my throat this way. What better place than my childhood bedroom?"

Her hands moved to her chest and plucked her nipples. It was useless to fight it, my eyes dropped to the way her rosy tips looked between her small fingers. I liked the way they looked better between my larger, rougher ones. My feet moved of their own volition, until I stood by her head, looking down her lean, beautiful body.

"Defile me," she begged, almost breaking me. Her hand slid up my thigh to cup my balls, rolling them in her palm. "You can be rough with my tiny throat," she said in a small voice, pouting over the words. "Force me to swallow your fat cock. Make me choke on all your cum. I've never had a dick in my mouth before."

I was rock hard and about to burst through the zipper of my slacks. With a dexterity that amazed me, she undid my buckle and pants.

"This is so fucking wrong, Olivia. I'm not some predator."

She breathed a laugh, the soft air caressing the underside of my length, completely comfortable with playing the role of a little girl submitting to a grown man. Meanwhile, my body and head were at war. I ached to do as she said and bury myself inside her, but my mind screamed how wrong it was. I'd done a lot of role-playing, but never this.

"I never said you were." She leaned up and flicked her tongue along my shaft. "Besides, it's not the actual scene that has me soaking through my panties, it's the forbidden—the taboo—that's making me ache."

"Fuck," I growled and gave in. "Open your mouth, little girl. I'm going to teach you how to suck my dick."

Pushing my head to her lips, her mouth fell open, and I eased my way in. I'd pushed to her throat before but never like this. Never in a way, I could see the head of my cock bulging in her throat each time I pushed all the way in.

Olivia held on to my ass with one hand and played with her tits with the other, making the most delicious choking sounds. Leaning back, I looked down at her stretched mouth, tears streaming down her face. Her hand dug harder into my ass, and that consent was enough to have me falling headfirst into this game she started.

Resting my fingers on her neck, I felt the way it stretched around my head. "Your throat is too little for my fat cock. But you'll take it, won't you?"

She whimpered, playing her role but followed it with a humming vibration. Wanting her to come too, I leaned over and tugged her panties aside, sliding my fingers through her wet slit, rolling them across her swollen clit.

"Look at this tight young pussy, all wet from sucking a man's dick. Has anyone touched you here before?"

She shook her head no and squeezed her legs closed, but I pried them apart.

"I don't think so. I'm going to finger this tiny pussy until you're screaming around my thick cock. You're going to swallow all my cum and like it."

Her hips went wild, and I continued to push in and out of her mouth, almost coming along with her when she struggled to scream her pleasure.

I stood upright again and cradled her neck, fucking her hard now, ready to come.

"That's it, little girl. Let me use that pretty mouth to spill my cum in. Take it. When I'm done, you'll be begging me to let you suck me again." I fingered her throat again. "I wish I could take a picture of the head of my cock stretching this little girl throat. I wish I could make you watch back how a grown man defiled you, taking his pleasure from your body."

With a few more thrusts, with all her stuffed animals atop her pink bedspread, her pompoms perched on a shelf, I emptied myself into Olivia's throat.

"Fucking swallow it. All of it," I moaned.

I pushed as far in as I could go and almost collapsed from the pleasure as pulse after pulse of my cum spilled down her throat.

Slipping out, Olivia coughed a few times but quickly went back to suck any remaining cum from the head. She rolled over to her knees, only in her skirt, her perky breasts rosy and still hard, her mascara streaking down her cheeks from her tears. Cradling her face, I wiped my thumb through the black lines, smearing them more. "Fucking beautiful."

She smiled with pride, and despite her confidence, I still questioned mine.

"I've never fantasized about that," I confessed. "And you know I'm not with you because of how young you are, right?"

She rose up and wrapped her arms around my neck, laying a gentle kiss to my lips. She was soothing me like I hadn't just roughly fucked her throat. This woman was amazing.

"I know that, Kent. It's just a fantasy—one I *have* thought about. Not that I'm with you because of your age, because I'm not. There's nothing wrong with fantasies. Maybe one night, I can convince you to sneak into my apartment and force me."

I groaned in pleasure and pain. "You're going to kill me."

"It's all consensual," she said with an easy shrug as though she hadn't admitted how much she trusted me to do a rape fantasy with her.

I pulled her tight, burying my head in her neck. "God, I love you."

"I love you too."

I'd never get tired of hearing those words.

"You should probably go, so no one comes looking."

"Good idea." One last kiss and a flick of her nipples, and I pulled back, tucking myself away. "Night, baby."

"Goodnight, Kent."

I shut the door softly and crept down the stairs thinking of reasons for being gone for fifteen minutes. The only excuse I had was embarrassing, but worth it for what I'd just done with Olivia.

"You get lost?" Daniel joked.

"No. Something just isn't sitting right with me." I laughed and laid my hand on my stomach.

Daniel cringed and tossed the remaining amber liquid down his throat. "Maybe we should leave."

"Yeah, that's probably best."

I definitely needed to get out of there before I went back to Olivia's room and *really* defiled her.

23 OLIVIA

"Look who I found," Oaklyn deadpanned behind me.

I turned away from the computer to find Oaklyn and...

Fucking Aaron.

"Livvie-baby." He held his arms wide with a cheesy-ass smile that instantly annoyed me. "I couldn't miss lunch with my favorite girl."

Oaklyn's disgusted face almost made me want to laugh out loud at the situation if I wasn't sitting in the middle of Kent's hotel lobby, where Kent could appear any moment to see me talking with my used-to-be fuck-buddy. I quickly looked around as if Kent would pop around the corner at any moment and ran through all the ways I could get rid of Aaron without just kicking his ass out the door.

Two lanky arms wrapped around me, and I immediately pulled out of his arms as gently as possible to avoid a scene.

What the fuck? I mouthed to Oaklyn.

She shrugged with pursed lips, her eyes screaming, *I told you so,* about Aaron. "I was kind of hoping for just a girl's lunch," she said, trying to save us from any more time with the octopus, I was currently trying to escape.

"Livvie wants me here," Aaron defended, standing too close behind me.

"I'm looking right at her, and she looks thrilled." Oaklyn forced a smile to match her sarcastic tone, but it went over Aaron's head.

"Told you."

Ugh, what an idiot. I was rolling my eyes when I saw two tall men walk in. *Oh. Fuck. Me.*

Kent's eyes locked with mine, hardening to flint when he took in Aaron.

I took an exaggerated step away from Aaron, not bothering to hide my annoyance when he smiled down at me.

Seeing him here, standing in Kent's hotel, I barely held off a shudder. How did I screw around with him as long as I did? Oaklyn was right, I did deserve better, and tracking Kent across the lobby, I knew I'd found it. Being with him—loving him—had me realizing I'd only kept Aaron around to control him and the relationship I decided to have with him. I couldn't get hurt if I didn't open up, and nothing about Aaron encouraged me to open up.

"Listen, Aar—"

"Is that my favorite niece slaving away?" Daniel said, interrupting my attempt to politely tell Aaron to fuck off.

"Hey, Uncle Daniel."

He walked over and wrapped me in his arms, thankfully, putting more distance between Aaron and me. And Oaklyn, the goddess she was, took the opportunity to stand between us too, her eyes letting me know how fucked up this whole situation was.

It was like the beginning of some bad joke. A girl walks into the bar and sees her past fuck-buddy, current lover, and uncle all smiling at her. What does a girl do? If I had a choice, I'd have loved it if a hole would've opened up and swallowed me alive. I would have loved for Kent to wrap his arms around me and tell Aaron to fuck off and then have lunch with him.

None of that happened.

The disappointment of it not happening mixed with the gratitude that Kent held himself back in front of Daniel. And then, there was the guilt at creating a situation where he couldn't stake his claim. But right now, wasn't the time.

"We were just about to have some lunch," Oaklyn said.

"Fantastic, so were we." Daniel smiled but eyed Aaron skeptically. "Kent had lunch ordered in for everyone, I'm sure a few extra friends can join, right, buddy?"

"Sure," Kent managed from his clenched jaw.

We made our way to the mostly empty conference room. A few people still lingered, finishing up their breaks. Daniel and Kent sat on one side of the table, and we sat on the other. Unfortunately, Aaron snagged a seat right next to me, but I did my best to make it clear I was scooting away.

"Are you the uncle that owns the sex club?" Aaron asked around a mouthful of food.

"No," Daniel answered with a dead stare.

"Oh..." Aaron's eyebrows furrowed and turned his confused gaze to me. "How many uncles do you have?"

"Just Daniel."

I would've laughed at his confusion if I wasn't so desperate for him to just be fucking gone.

"It's not a sex club," Daniel explained. His tone was casual, with a hint of irritation bubbling underneath. "Just a regular club."

Aaron still looked baffled by Daniel's explanation until his mouth dropped open into an "ooooooohhh" like a lightbulb had just gone off. "I see," he said with an exaggerated wink. Now *I* was confused. "Got to keep it on the down-low."

Oaklyn stopped chewing to give Aaron her full what-the-fuck stare. I didn't blame her. He was such an idiot.

"I'd love to get in there," Aaron continued, completely unaware of everyone's annoyance at his presence. It was only a matter of moments before Kent's death-glare finally dropped Aaron dead. "Maybe you could get your niece and her boyfriend in. Olivia and I could have a date." He gave another wink and bobbed his eyebrows at me.

"Barf," Oaklyn said.

"No," Daniel and Kent said at the same time.

"You're not my boyfriend," I said over all of them.

"C'mon, Livvie," Aaron tried to cajole.

"Just shut up, Aaron."

"Okay, okay." He held up his hands in surrender. "I know how it is."

I glared, on the brink of punching him. This room was a mess getting worse by the second, and I needed a moment's reprieve before I snapped. "I'll be back."

I DARTED my eyes across the table to Kent, who hadn't taken his eyes off Aaron. Then, I chanced a look at Daniel, and a small part of me crumpled under his confused gaze. One eyebrow rose like he was asking me if this was who I really wanted in my life. I wanted to shout across the table that no, it wasn't and beg him to forget this ever happened. Anything to get rid of the tinge of disappointment coloring the questioning look.

It was so minute, but enough to dig deep and make it hard to breathe—like a needle in my lungs. I needed to get out of that room. I needed a moment away from all the ways I could make Daniel disappointed in me at one tiny table.

As soon as I stood, Aaron cut in again with a new topic that had me freezing at the door.

"Aren't you going to be speaking at our class, Mr. Kent? Just got the email today."

I turned with wide eyes, but as soon as my gaze clashed with his, he looked away. "Yes. Professor Arden contacted me earlier this week."

Part of me wanted to stay and ask more questions like, why hadn't he told me. But my body urged me to get the fuck out of that room before I screamed.

I was washing my hands when the door opened.

His dark gaze pinned me in place through the mirror. My fingers dug into the cold marble of the sink when he pressed his front to my back, pushing my hips against the counter. He gripped my waist and leaned down to burrow his nose in my hair, inhaling deeply. Such a simple move that sent chills down my spine, igniting a fire between my thighs. I couldn't help the moan that slipped free and the way I arched back, rubbing my ass against his growing erection.

"Do you know how hard it is?" I rubbed my ass against him again. "To watch that disgusting little prick act like he has a right to you?" His hand moved up past my breasts to wrap around my throat, fingering the silver chain. "To act like he has a right to what is *mine*."

I waited until his gaze met mine.

"Yes. I would murder any woman who tried to touch you," I admitted because it was the truth, and it was the least I could give him after that charade out there. "I'm sorry. I'm yours."

His eyes flashed with regret before his hand moved to fist my hair. I gasped when he jerked hard enough to sting my scalp deliciously. I held still, letting him kiss his way up my neck to nip at my ear, all while he bunched my skirt up higher and higher to reach my pussy.

I tried to push back again, wanting to feel as much of him as possible, but he tugged my hair in reprimand, his hand burrowing in my panties to cup me.

"Mine," he growled.

"All yours. Promise. All yours."

My knees almost gave out when his finger slipped between my folds and played with my clit.

"Kent," I whimpered. "Fuck me. Please."

"Right here? In the bathroom?" he taunted, playing at my opening.

"Right here. Give it to me."

Desperation had me releasing my fist from the counter, and reaching back to grip his shaft, stroking him hard, loving his grunt.

"Fuck, I missed you."

I continued to stroke him, and he moved to divest me of my panties. They had just cleared my ass when the bathroom door flew open.

Oaklyn's wide eyes met mine through the mirror before one eyebrow slowly rose into her hairline. She didn't say anything as she made her way to the stall. "You may want to hurry up. Daniel is looking for you," she said before disappearing behind the door.

Kent tugged my underwear back in place. "Later. Meet me here later."

"Always," I promised.

Part of me wanted to walk out of the bathroom with his hand in mine, but I knew today wasn't the day.

Once we were both presentable, he placed one more kiss to my lips and walked out. I leaned against the counter and waited for Oaklyn.

"That was bold," she said, washing her hands.

I shrugged. "Please tell me Aaron is gone."

Her smirk gave me an answer before she did. "He's waiting for his *Livvie-baby*."

"Blech."

"God, Olivia. Just tell him to fuck off."

"I know. I wasn't going to. But I feel like it's going to take a sign and an ultra-big blow to his ego to get through that thick skull of his, and I didn't want to do that here where I'm working."

"I will happily paint a sign tonight and hit him in the head with it," she offered.

"Such a good friend," I laughed.

"Come on. Let's go before Daniel murders A-a-ron."

"That would solve my problem," I said wistfully.

Turned out, my problem was solved because Aaron was walking out the door.

"Said he had to go," Kent explained with a smirk.

I could imagine what he'd said to make him leave.

"That guy is a douche, Olivia," Daniel sneered. "Don't date him."

"Good thing I'm not then. He's not my boyfriend."

"Keep it that way," Kent murmured.

Daniel patted Kent on the back. "See, I love having her here with you. I know she's safe with you keeping an eye on her, and away from all the perverts like that."

Oaklyn coughed next to me but turned away before I could give her my full glare.

A muscle ticked in Kent's jaw, and he nodded toward the door. "Come on, D. Let's go meet Carina and sign these papers."

My heart sunk when he avoided my gaze. I knew he wasn't happy that he had to pretend around Daniel. I knew I was screwing this up, but I didn't know how to fix it. I didn't know how to believe it wouldn't explode in my face.

I didn't know how to have faith that Daniel wouldn't see me as everyone else did, and nothing I could say would fix it. And maybe when he saw me for what I truly was, he'd make Kent see me that way too.

God, I wanted to sink to the floor, disappointed in myself. Here I was walking around all proud, strong, and aloof, and the reality was that Olivia Witt was a big fat scaredy-cat.

The reality was that I had two men who saw me, and I didn't want to disappoint either one, and the further I got into this, I didn't know how to get to the other side without losing both.

24 KENT

"I'm seeing someone."

Everyone at the table froze. I almost laughed at the picture they made.

My mom was the first one to lift wide eyes to mine. My dad's eyes quickly following. Jacob held a fork halfway to his mouth, his lips slowly stretching into a smirk. The undying support of my sister-in-law, Lily, smiled like a proud mom as she perched my niece, Ava, in her lap who had even stopped squeezing mashed potatoes through her fat fists.

Jacob broke the silence first. "Like once?"

I glared across the table. "Like seriously, asshole."

"Language," Mom reprimanded. Her eyes darted over to Ava, who had resumed playing in her food.

"I think it's about time," Lily said.

She always told me it was a matter of time, I just needed to find the right woman. My brother found it hilarious that she was so dead-set on me falling in love. Especially when I hadn't even been looking to settle down.

I returned Lily's smile, feeling good to have someone's support and confidence.

Somewhere along the drive to our family dinner, I decided to tell someone about Olivia. Maybe saying it out loud to someone would help with not being able to say it out loud to Daniel. I also knew I couldn't stand much longer without punching anyone who dared to look at what was mine.

"Well, why didn't you bring her?" my mom asked.

A knot eased in my chest at her raised eyebrow. Sharing my relationship with Olivia felt like handling a bomb. You were careful with it, but in the wrong hands, it could go off in your face. And like Mom always did, she handled everything with care.

"I want to meet the woman who can make you stop for more than a date since Ivette."

"She's busy tonight."

I toyed with the idea of bringing her, but she'd had to study for an exam and prepare a presentation.

Because she was a college student. A twenty-one-year-old college student. That was seventeen years younger than me.

The knot that had eased a moment ago twisted again. I could sit here and pretend that the worst part was announcing that I had a girlfriend, but what would their reaction be when I told them how young she was?

"Well, don't make us drag it out of you," my dad said. "What's she like?"

An easy smile stretched my lips just thinking about her. "She's beautiful, of course, but she's also so full of life. She's smart and tenacious, always going after what she wants. She definitely keeps me in line with her smart mouth."

"Someone needs to," Jacob murmured.

I ignored his comment. "She's also ready for anything. Just as excited to try new things as I am. Challenging me to push harder. She makes me a better man."

Mom's hand was pressed to her lips. She had that look that could only be described as a proud mom look everyone knew and loved. The one that you got when you scored a goal in soccer, when you graduated college, when you opened your first hotel, and apparently when you fell in love.

"She sounds like a much better fit for you than Ivette," Dad said.

Mom shook her head. "That woman was too controlling and not a good match for your free spirit."

"That woman had a stick up her ass," Jacob said.

"Language," both Lily and Mom reprimanded.

Jacob held his hands up in surrender.

"I can't wait to meet her," Mom said.

"I can't wait either."

The thought of Olivia at this long formal table filled with laughter and love had my heart stretched too big in the confines of my chest. She'd slide perfectly into my life. I ached to have her here, but all that excitement at imagining her by my side was always dimmed by the complications of our relationship. I wanted to ignore them, but the deeper we got, the harder it became to pretend nothing stood between us.

"Make sure you bring her next time," Mom ordered.

I swallowed, and my smile slipped. "Of course, Mom. She'd love to come."

I was sure my hesitation was too quick to notice, except when I looked across the table, Jacob was staring back, questions written all over his face, and I knew I wasn't getting home without him grilling me.

Conversation moved on to everyone else around the table, and I managed to avoid Jacob's interrogation until each of us had a beer in hand, sitting in the rocking chairs on the back porch. He let me enjoy the night for a moment, looking out over Mom's dimly lit oasis she'd created in our large backyard.

I was about halfway done with my beer when he finally spoke up.

"So, what's wrong?"

Deny, deny, deny.

"Nothing's wrong."

His stare burned into the side of my head. "Really? Because as soon as Mom brought up bringing this mysterious woman who's ensnared you, you shut down."

"Nerves, I guess. Haven't brought anyone home since Ivette."

"Bullshit. Fess up."

I drained the rest of my beer and held off answering, as long as I could. These doubts and concerns over Olivia and I had been locked inside, and I hadn't realized until that moment how much I needed to say them out loud. I needed someone to tell me I wasn't insane for loving her. Usually, the person I'd go to was Daniel, but obviously, that was out of the question.

So, letting it all come out to Jacob sounded damn good right then.

"She's twenty-one."

Jacob choked on his beer, lunging forward, so he didn't spill on himself as he coughed up a lung.

I clenched my jaw while he was folded in half, a mixture of coughing and laughter shaking his body.

"No wonder she's full of life. She's a baby."

"She's not a baby," I ground out.

Jacob wiped his eyes and finally looked up to find how serious this was to me. "You really do care about her."

My heart rolled around in my chest. "More than any woman I've been with."

He leaned back with a groan, swiping his hand across his

face. "Listen, Alex. If she makes you happy, then so be it. You're both adults, and it doesn't matter what people think."

Some of the weight crushing my chest lifted, and I breathed in the crisp night air.

"Besides, Mom always wanted another granddaughter."

He scooted his chair back, barely missing the slap to the side of the head, I reached to deliver. "Fuck off," I growled. But I also smiled, not able to help myself from joining in on Jacob's laughter.

A few more minutes passed, and I had to decide whether to be completely honest or to enjoy the relief of Jacob's approval. In the end, I knew I'd be confessing all my sins. I wasn't a man to hide from admitting my faults, and I didn't want to hide behind a half-truth to make myself feel better.

"There's one more thing. She's D's niece." Jacob's chair stopped rocking, but I didn't look to see his expression. I knew it couldn't be anything good. "And she doesn't want to tell him."

The silence stretched on until I thought I would scream just to break it, but before I could snap, his chair began rocking again.

"You are truly fucked."

Damn. I'd hoped for anything other than confirmation that this was a goddamn mess.

"I know," I admitted wearily.

"Is this just a fling? Maybe some daddy issues?"

"No," I grumbled. "She doesn't have daddy issues. Why would you say that?"

"Because she's twenty-one, Kent. I couldn't settle on what I wanted for dinner at twenty-one, let alone a solid relationship."

"Mom and Dad were high school sweethearts," I argued.

"Yeah, and they were both young. They grew together. You're almost forty—settled. Is she going to want to settle with you when she grows into adulthood?"

Of all the issues that laid between us, her changing into

someone I didn't fit with never crossed my mind. We had too many other external forces working against us, I never looked beyond them.

I couldn't deny his words. Jacob wasn't wrong.

"Fuck," I breathed.

"Yeah. Fuck."

"I just never thought about it."

"I can see that."

"She's solid though. She's confident in who she is. She's not an immature girl searching for herself. I know that."

And I did. Yes, his worries were valid, but only from someone who didn't know the woman Olivia was. Despite his concern, I was confident in her—in us.

"Then there's just one question you have to ask yourself."

"What?"

"Is she worth it? Even if it all falls apart. Would she be worth it?"

Olivia's playful smile and devious smirk flashed through my mind. The way she threw her head back and laughed, her blonde hair spilling down her back. The way my heart beat twice as hard when I walked into the hotel to find her sharing her brilliant ideas. The way my mind calmed as soon as she was in my arms. The way her eyes always dared me for more.

God, I loved her.

"Yeah, she's worth it."

"Good, because she may be all you have by your side after telling Daniel you're fucking his baby niece," Jacob said with a laugh.

Losing Daniel was the least of my worries.

What scared me more was even if we did tell Daniel, she'd still leave me.

And no matter how much I wanted to deny it, the fear planted itself deep.

25 KENT

"I REALLY APPRECIATE YOU COMING, Mr. Kent," Elizabeth Arden said, opening the door to the auditorium.

"It's an honor to come and speak to our future entrepreneurs."

"*Hopefully,* our future entrepreneurs. I'm not sure all of them will make it." She sat her books and papers down and leaned against the wooden desk to face me. "Miss Witt seems like she'll be one of the ones to make it."

My heart galloped harder and squeezed in on itself all at once at the mention of Olivia's name. We weren't doing anything wrong, but I was sure a student fucking the man helping with a school project would be heavily frowned upon.

"I would expect nothing less," I managed with a smooth tone.

"I was worried she would end up failing this class. She was very apathetic when she started, but once she began interning for your business, she seemed revived and more excited than I'd ever seen her."

"She's very talented. I—my company was very lucky to have her help."

Dr. Arden's hair fell forward when she looked down and laughed. "Yes, she bragged a bit about her ideas being utilized."

I looked down too, to hide the smile I knew gave away my adoration. When I looked up, Dr. Arden was taking me in, biting her lip. "Maybe we can grab lunch after this if you're free."

She was a beautiful woman close to my age. This time last year, I would have jumped at the chance to fuck this woman, taken the opportunity to play out any teacher fantasies I had. But not anymore. Now, the idea of changing from one woman to the next sounded exhausting. If I had any teacher fantasies, I knew Olivia would be more than happy to play them out.

"I appreciate the offer, but I have to get back to the office before flying out."

If she was embarrassed by my rejection, she didn't show it. She simply shrugged a shoulder. "Of course." Standing from her position, she turned to shuffle through some papers. "Feel free to set up whatever you need. The students should be piling in any minute."

On cue, the door opened, and they trickled in. I did my best to not search for Olivia, but I didn't need to bother. The energy around me changed when she was near, like her body called to mine. She held my gaze for only a moment. Just long enough to make sure I saw the way her tongue slicked across her lips, and the way she scanned me head to toe.

My cock hardened, and I shifted to stand behind the lectern to hide what she did to me. I struggled to get my arousal under control when she sat in the front row and kept running her fingers along her exposed collarbone just under the silver chain. She wore a floral print dress that teased around her thighs with thin straps. She had on a thick cardigan, but she let it slide off her shoulder, and even that simple flash of skin had me wanting to bite her—mark her there, so everyone knew she was mine.

Especially when that pencil-dick little twerp plopped down

next to her and couldn't take his eyes off her cleavage. Olivia glared, and tugged the sweater back up, scooting away as much as she could in her tiny seat.

Dr. Arden introduced me, and I began my speech about how I got into business and my success with it. The entire time, my emotions swayed from raging jealousy, wanting to rip A-a-ron apart to heated desire imagining fucking her in front of everyone.

By the time we made it to the Q and A, my dick was stretching the limits of my pants.

I became even more turned on when Olivia glared at each girl who asked a question overtly flirting with me.

"Do you make sure to test all the beds in each of your hotels to make sure they have enough...bounce?"

"How do you make sure the furniture is sturdy enough for any *rough* visitors?"

I didn't know why I was surprised by their bold questions considering Olivia had pursued me rather overtly, but answering them felt like walking through a minefield. I was grateful when Dr. Arden let us know class was over.

"I have to run," Dr. Arden said. "Take your time. No one uses this room for the rest of the day."

With a few more thank yous, she was gone.

Some of the girls lingered, but when I didn't pay them any attention, they quickly left. Olivia took her sweet time packing up her notebooks, ensuring she was one of the last to leave the room. When the class was almost empty, she made her approach. She'd just opened her mouth when Pencil-dick threw his arm around her shoulders and tugged her close.

"How's our girl doing, Alex?"

My whole body clenched, watching his arm around *my* woman. The fact that he was an arrogant prick addressing me like he knew me was only icing on the rage-filled cake. My muscles ached from restraining to not pulverize a fucking student.

I didn't even register Olivia's reaction, I was so consumed with coming up with ways to murder Aaron and hide his body. When I was sure I could get away with it, I took a step forward. But just as I did, Olivia reacted.

She twisted her shoulders and ducked under his arm, shoving him for good measure. "I'm not your girl, Aaron," she snarled. "I can't believe how disrespectful you're being right now. Especially in front of Mr. Kent."

Aaron, undeterred and apparently missing the warning signs that he might not make it out of this room in one piece, stepped back into Olivia's space. "You may not be my *girl,*" he said with air quotes. "But you're my Netflix and chill. I'm sure Alex understands. He was in college once."

That was it. He was dead. My hand was already lifting when Olivia side-stepped to get between Aaron and me.

"What *Mr. Kent,*" she said, enunciating my name, "did in college doesn't matter. What matters is that you stop touching me." She stepped forward, and Aaron must have read something on her face because, for the first time, he backed up. "Stop assuming I'm yours. Stop calling me. Matter of fact, *A-a-ron,* just stop remembering I exist and fuck off."

Pencil-dick swallowed, and I barely held back my laugh at him being so scared of this fireball in front of him. It didn't take him long to recover though. He pulled his shoulders back and screwed up his face. "Whatever. Your loss."

And with that, he was gone. Hopefully, forever.

Olivia's shoulders rose and fell on a deep breath before she turned to me with an embarrassed twist to her lips. "Sorry about that."

My first reaction was to pull her in my arms and tell her how proud I was of her being a badass, but somehow, I held back. Instead, I reacted with the desire and need that had been brewing for the past hour. "Close the door," I ordered.

Her eyes widened, and color rose on her cheeks. "Kent, we can't."

"Did I ask for your permission?"

"No," she breathed.

"Then go close the door."

She swallowed, turning to do as she was told. By the time she turned back to me, I stood beside the teacher's desk, waiting for her.

"Come here."

Her steps were almost silent as she crossed the room until she stood inches from me. Her tongue slicked across her full lips, and I fought from leaning in to bite them, to suck her tongue into my mouth and taste her.

"Put your hands on the desk," I ordered.

She looked so innocent with her wide blue eyes, smooth skin, and the classroom behind her. It shouldn't have turned me on as much as it did, but I couldn't help it. All that innocence masked the wild, erotic woman beneath. She placed her hands on the edge of the desk and adjusted her hips, widening her legs without even being told. She presented her ass perfectly.

She jumped when my fingers caressed the back of her thigh but didn't move. Up, up, up, my hand trailed, leaving goosebumps in their wake until I reached the plump curve of her ass. I delicately lifted the skirt of her dress and rested it above her hips. Her white lace panties only half covered the pale cheeks. I stroked the skin, massaged her in my hand, never reaching between her legs, no matter how much she squirmed.

"Kent," she breathed.

Smack.

The crack against her ass vibrated through the room, immediately followed by her yelp and then a moan.

Smack, smack, smack.

I rained down quick slaps, covering each pale inch with the

red mark of my hand. Stopping to take time to smooth out the burn, only to spank her again. By the time I was done, she was whimpering and rubbing her thighs together, but I quickly gripped her hips and kicked her feet out, making room for myself between her thighs.

I dragged my hand down and cupped her wet pussy, holding tight. "You are mine," I growled against the back of her neck. I needed to hear the confirmation, even if it was redundant. Watching Aaron's hands on her, my brother's doubts, the chance of losing her—all of it weighed on me, and I just wanted to hear her say it.

"I'm yours."

It was the only confirmation I needed before tugging her panties aside, and freeing my cock, not waiting a second before pushing all the way in. We both groaned, finally relieved to take care of the ache that had been consuming us the past hour. We'd stopped using condoms, and each time I entered her, her wet heat brought me to the edge.

"Hold on, baby."

Her knuckles turned white, gripping the desk, and I didn't hold back when I held her hips and fucked her ruthlessly.

"Kent," she whimpered. "What if someone comes in?"

"Let them," I said through clenched teeth. "Let them see me claiming you. Let them watch me fuck you—leaving my mark on you. Then everyone will know that you are mine."

Reaching around, I swirled my fingers around her clit fast and hard. As much as I didn't care if someone caught me balls deep inside her, I knew she would. So, I set about making her come fast.

Her hand slapped over her mouth to hold back her screams as her pussy squeezed my cock, pulling my own orgasm from me. I leaned over her back, and bit at her shoulder, groaning my pleasure, spilling my cum inside her.

"Fuck, I love you so much," I whispered, peppering kisses along her back. She turned her head and met me halfway to meet my lips.

"I love you too."

I eased out of her and cleaned us both up with the handkerchief I kept in my suit pocket.

Once she righted her dress, she turned to face me, and I jerked her into my arms for another kiss.

"Not that I'm complaining, but what's got you so hot and bothered. Other than me, of course."

I dragged my nose along hers and pressed my forehead to hers. "Watching Aaron even talk to you, and not be able to pull you close killed me."

"I wasn't too thrilled with all those girls hanging on your every word."

"You would be able to rub it in their faces if you'd just admit we're together." I hadn't meant the words to come out so harsh, but I was reaching the end of my rope. Each time I saw Daniel, a noose hung around my neck, just waiting to be pulled tight. I hated lying to him. "Have you even tried to talk to Daniel?"

"I—I haven't had the time."

"Then give up a night with me and tell him."

"I—Kent."

Pulling out of our embrace, my heart sank when she wouldn't meet my eyes. Her tongue slicked across her lips as she studied the ground, her hands clenching and unclenching by her side. "Olivia."

"I just need time."

"I've given you time." My words echoed around the empty room.

Her eyes jerked to mine, and the bright blue, I loved so much, glossed over. "It's not that easy."

"Actually, it is that easy. You want to be an adult, then make the hard decision to get what you want. Stop playing this dumb girl to get your way."

She stood there, eyes wide, not saying anything like she expected me to take it back. But I wouldn't. She was mature enough to handle everything, she didn't get to pick and choose what she showed up for and what she hid behind her façade to avoid.

When I remained silent, she pulled her shoulders back and stood tall, pulling her armor around her. "Is that what you think of me? That I'm some dumb girl?"

"No, Olivia. It's the fact that I know you *aren't* some dumb girl that pisses me off that you keep acting like it when it comes time to tell Daniel."

Her chest rose and fell over her heavy breathing, but her lips remained pinched tight.

"Olivia, I love you—"

"Then let that be enough," she interrupted. But I continued like I hadn't heard her.

"But I can't keep lying to Daniel. I'm almost forty. I don't hide who I am."

Her eyes flicked around the room as if she'd find an answer written on the walls. Eventually, she looked back to me, her eyes defiant, but I could see the plea in them too. "I can't, Kent. And I'm asking you to be okay with that."

My eyes slid closed, trying to pull back on the hurt and anger surging up, but when they opened, it was all still there. The love of my life, standing there, asking me to lie. It was too much to hold back. "I won't keep lying to him, and you remember what happened to the last woman who asked me to lie," I said dangerously low.

Olivia stumbled back like I'd hit her, and I regretted the comparison to my ex-wife. I regretted implying I'd leave her just as easily. We were so much more than what Ivette and I had been.

I ran a hand through my hair and was about to take the words back, when she squared her shoulders again, and slid a coat of armor around her, blocking out any emotion from coming through. "You should go."

"I don't want to leave like this."

"There's a lot of things you don't want to do, but right now, I need you to walk away."

"At least let me walk you out."

"Please, Kent." Her voice cracked, and I saw through the hard veneer she was barely holding on to. She just needed time to cool down, and we would figure it out later when emotions were running less high.

"Will you meet me at the hotel later? I'm leaving tomorrow morning."

"I don't think that's a good idea. I'm not sure any of this is a good idea."

Her words hit me like a punch to the gut, sucking all the air from my lungs. "Olivia," I pleaded. We could work past this.

I loved her.

We loved each other.

"Please, just go."

When I still stood there, dumbfounded by the rapid turn of events, she grabbed her things and walked out, leaving me behind.

26 OLIVIA

I EXITED the cab in front of the hotel and stared up at the tall building. Five days—the longest I'd been away from the hotel since I started over three months ago, and I missed it. But I was done here. I would finish my project next week, I just needed to grab some final information from Vivian, and I'd have no reason to come back.

I was happy at the same time as dreading it.

I was happy to finish the project. Relieved to not have to face Kent every day and miss him. I dreaded leaving because I'd lose the connection I had to something that had made me excited about my future. I dreaded leaving because I'd lose the connection I had to *him*.

He'd messaged me a few times a day since I'd walked out on him, but I ignored each one. I wasn't even sure what to say or what I wanted him to say. Well, I knew what I wanted him to say; *I was wrong.* The reality was that the only person who needed to be saying that was me.

And I couldn't because, over the past five days, nothing had changed. Panic crashed over me, stealing my breath, each time I thought of using it to tell Daniel the truth. Maybe I was just the dumb, scared girl he accused of being a façade.

Taking a deep breath, I prepared for whatever stood on the other side of those doors. I knew he was back from New York, but I didn't know if he was here. Honestly, I wasn't sure what I was hoping to find.

I scanned each inch that I could, holding my breath around every corner until I found Vivian bent over some papers with one of the employees.

"Olivia." She stood and smiled. "I've missed you."

"I've missed you too. How has it been this week?"

"Fantastic. All the final touches are getting done this month, and then we open."

"That's so exciting."

"All our hard work, coming to fruition. We couldn't have done it without you."

"Thank you, Vivian," I said, smiling harder than I had in days.

"Oh, I wanted to ask you while Alexander is gone, his birthday is in a couple weeks, and we were going to throw him a little party in the hotel restaurant. It wouldn't be the same if you weren't there."

His birthday was soon? How had I not known?

The idea of a party with Kent had me mentally scrolling through my wardrobe, trying to find the sexiest dress to tempt him. It all came to a screeching halt when I thought about Daniel being there and Kent having to pretend I didn't exist.

Just like that, the stone in my stomach was back. "I'll see what I have going on," I answered noncommittally. "Is he here?"

"You just missed him. He had a flight to catch."

"Oh."

Vivian took me around to say goodbye and answered the few

questions I had. We were in one of the offices, packing up when she stopped me.

"Miss Russo wanted me to give you this."

I looked down at the packet of papers she had. "What is it?"

She gestured for me to read, and I scanned the top.

Internship Application for
Wellington and Russo Marketing Team.

"Oh...Wow. I..."

"She specifically said you were her top pick and hoped you'd filled it out."

Tears burned the backs of my eyes, and I had to blink to hold them at bay.

"You'll be a shoo-in, Olivia, with all your talent."

"Thank you," I breathed, overwhelmed by her kind words.

Daniel always told me I was smart, that I had crazy talent, but these last couple years, I'd walked around flippant about my future and letting people believe I was a spoiled airhead. I had no reason to prove otherwise, no one else expected anything else. Maybe part of me began believing it to be true.

But after this project, I felt a drive like I hadn't before. To have Carina Russo say that she wanted me, locked that ambition in place, and I couldn't wait to get home and fill it out.

"Well, sweetie. I have to go make some phone calls. I'll see you around. Hopefully, at the party." She stepped around the corner and jerked back, her hand to her chest. "Goodness, Alexander. You scared me," she laughed, walking past him.

"Sorry about that, Viv. Thankfully, I remembered I forgot some papers before I made it to the airport."

I thought I'd make it out without seeing him. I thought I'd get a reprieve, but just hearing the deep rumble of his voice from around the door had my heart tripping over itself to get to him.

When he rounded the corner and saw me standing there, he froze, and I fought every muscle in my body to not run to him. His beard was thicker than before, and he looked tired.

"Olivia."

Just my name, but it stroked across my skin, trying to seduce me into his arms. When I didn't move, he closed the door and stepped closer, only stopping when I took a step back. His eyes pinched closed as if in pain before opening. I could at least be kind enough to not lead him on.

"How are you?"

"Fine."

"You've ignored my calls."

"I've been busy."

The muscle along his jaw jumped. "Don't lie, Olivia," he ground out.

My lungs squeezed too tight to take a deep breath. He'd inched closer and sucked all the air from my lungs, refusing to give it back until I gave him what he wanted. I just didn't know that I could. "What do you want me to say, Kent?"

Another step. "I want you to tell me the truth. I want you to come here and be in my arms. I want you to let me love you."

He made it all sound so easy.

"You know I love you." I wouldn't pretend everything would work out, but I, at least, wouldn't lie about how I felt about him. No amount of time dimmed that love.

"Olivia."

"I'm sorry."

That muscle jumped again, and he tried to hold my gaze, but his dropped before popping back up filled with the answer I was tired of hearing.

"Then, nothing has changed." It wasn't a question.

I tried to step around him, but his hands framed my face and held me close. "Please, don't do this."

Please don't make me stay here and see what my fear was holding me back from.

I stared into his deep brown eyes, remembering how much they'd entranced me when we first met at Voyeur. Who knew one night would end like this? *Was* this the end? Was this the last time I'd ever look up and want to sink into his gaze?

Wanting to take the chance while I had it, I pressed to my toes and almost had my lips to his when his phone vibrated in his pocket.

"Shit," he muttered. "That's my driver. I have a plane waiting."

I sank back to my feet and nodded.

"I have to go. He leaned down, speaking the words against my lips. His mouth moved like a whisper, barely there, almost imagined. "I'll call you when I land."

Everything in me pushed to close the breath of a gap between us. But for once, in the presence of Kent, my mind won out, reminding me of why having his hands cradle me so gently hurt so much.

I stepped out of his reach. "Don't worry about it."

I hated myself, standing there watching his fists clench and unclench, letting my fear win out. Terrified, if I lost Daniel, I'd find nothing but a hollow bimbo underneath. Terrified of the world of hurt awaiting me when he finally walked away.

"Dammit, Olivia." His jaw clenched. "Listen. I'm here. If you want to talk, I'm here. Call. Message. Smoke signals. Anything."

The lump that had been residing in my chest since last week worked its way up my throat, and I was scared that if I opened my mouth, it would all come out—I would sob and beg him to not leave me. So, instead, I nodded.

He hesitated, his body stiff with indecision before he nodded back and turned, walking out the door. I made sure to memorize his broad shoulders, tapering down to the most perfect ass. I took in his swagger and imprinted it on my mind. Just in case I never saw it again.

He said he was there for me, but not how I needed him. And right now, I needed time to figure out what I could live with.

And what I couldn't.

27 OLIVIA

"I think I'm going to dye my hair pink." Oaklyn's voice barely registered.

"Sounds good." I didn't even bother to look up from picking at my nail polish.

It'd been almost two weeks since I'd walked away from Kent the first time. Less than a week since I spent my last day in his hotel. Less than a week since he'd walked away from me.

I had no need to see him anymore. Except that my body desperately ached for him. Except that I missed hearing his voice and watching him laugh. Except that missing him hung like a fog around me—a buffer keeping any happiness out.

It was dramatic—rationally, I knew that, but my heart didn't care. It was a dramatic bitch that said screw rationality.

I'd moped around and clung to my phone, typing message after message only to delete them. He knew where I stood, and as devastated as I was, I wouldn't beg. As much as I wanted to say I wouldn't beg because of pride, the reality was that I knew it wouldn't change anything.

I saw the same hurt in his eyes—the hope that we could work past this, that I would step up and make a better decision. I saw the plea for me to just be strong and tell Daniel about us. But as much as the hurt clung to me, so did the fear, and I couldn't bring myself to do it. It didn't matter how much he loved me, and I loved him, sometimes love wasn't enough.

Which left me sitting in Callum and Oaklyn's living room, crossed legged, staring at my hands, picking at the last of my nail polish. I hated fidgeting. It showed weakness and nerves, and I was Olivia Witt. I didn't show any of those.

At least, I didn't used to. Now, that's all I was—a hollow body without the armor I used to wear before Kent.

"You're not even listening." Oaklyn's voice whipped through the fog.

Lifting my chin, I forced myself to meet her eyes. "Yes, I am," I lied.

She blinked slowly, giving me a deadpanned stare. "Really? Because I just said I was going to leave Cal to get a sex change, and I got nothing from you. No dick jokes or anything."

The reason I'd been avoiding her eyes in the first place hit me; the concern, the pity, the worry. If I could block them out, maybe I could pretend it was just me making a big deal out of nothing. But staring at Oaklyn now, there was no pretending this break up wasn't a devastating massacre.

"I'm sorry. I just...I'm a mess."

"I know."

"Thanks," I said dryly.

"You know what I mean. I hate that you're hurting, and I'm your best friend, so of course, I notice it no matter how much you hide." She reached across the cushion between us and held my hand, lowering her own gaze now. "Maybe it's better it happened now than later."

Her words hit me like a slap to the face, and I snatched my

hand away from hers. Oaklyn always played the devil's advocate for me as I did with her, but right then, I didn't need her rationale.

"There wasn't supposed to be a later," I argued. "Us breaking up shouldn't have happened *at all*."

She sat back and shook her head, not letting me hide behind the perfect future I'd pictured for Kent and I. Her look let me know she would drag out reality. Her look let me know she'd been soft and caring long enough, and it was time to face the truth. I both loved and hated her for what she was doing. I knew it would ground me and pull me back from my emotional ledge. I also knew it would hurt like a bitch.

"What did you expect to happen, Olivia? It was a lose-lose situation for him."

"I expected him to stand by me, no matter how long it took," I proclaimed, stabbing the couch. "I expected him to want me enough—to *love* me enough."

"Put yourself in his shoes. What if someone asked you to lie to me? Lie about something that could do irreparable damage if I discovered it on my own. Something that would hurt me to find out you lied about. The longer the lie goes on, the bigger the damage it can cause. He had just as much to lose as you if the lie continued."

"I know," I shouted. "I know. It just—it doesn't make it easier." My voice cracked on the last few words, and tears finally spilled down my cheeks. "I wouldn't want to lie to you either, but if I loved someone enough, I'd expect you to understand why I lied for so long. I'd expect you to understand."

Oaklyn scooted over and wrapped me in her arms, letting me bury my head against her shoulder and cry. She brushed her hand over my hair doing her best to soothe me.

"I'm so sorry, Olivia. I wish it was different for you. You were happier than I'd seen you in a while, and you know how much I wanted that for you."

"I wi-wish it was different t-too."

I clung to her, breaking down for the first time. Sure, I'd shed some tears and been angry at times, but I hadn't yet let it all come out, fearful of what would be left of me when it did.

Oddly enough, when the crying slowed, and my lungs could fully inhale again, I felt lighter and more full at once. It wasn't much, but for the first time, maybe it would be okay.

The front door opened, and Callum walked through, holding his briefcase. His large body looked comical frozen in the entryway, taking in the two of us hugging on the couch. His eyes widened, and his mouth opened like a fish out of water.

"Umm...I'm interrupting. I'm sorry."

He moved at lightning speed to shed his coat and place everything in the closet.

"It's okay, Dr. Pierce. I was just being dramatic all over Oaklyn. I'm done now."

His blue eyes flicked between us as I wiped the remnants of my breakdown from my face. "Okay," he said slowly, back to being frozen like a deer in headlights.

He could be so serious sometimes, and I had to admit, the thought of messing with him put back a piece I'd lost in the last two weeks. "Actually," I feigned more tears, "I could really use some more support. Do you think you could come hold me too?"

His eyes managed to widen even more. "Uhh, wh—" he cleared his throat when his voice cracked. "What?"

I pinched my lips together to hold back my laugh.

While I may have been able to hold it in, Oaklyn couldn't.

"Cal, I wish I could take a picture of your face. Olivia is just screwing with you."

He looked back at me and relaxed for the first time since stepping in when he found me shaking with laughter.

"Don't worry, you can go. We're almost done with our girl talk."

"Good to know."

And then he was gone so fast I was surprised he hadn't left skid marks in his wake. But just as quick, his head popped around the corner. "You staying for dinner?"

"Sure. That'd be great."

Dinner ended up being pasta delivered from a local restaurant. The food had been delicious, and Oaklyn had managed to make me laugh a time or two. By the end of the meal, I felt both better and the same. My body still ached, missing Kent with every move, but I also felt stronger like it was a load I could bear.

But when it came down to it, I didn't want to bear it. I wanted what Oaklyn and Callum had. They were the perfect picture of domesticated bliss—of what could become of a forbidden relationship. He'd been her professor and older than her, and yet they made it work.

"Do you have any plans for break, Olivia?" Callum asked, pulling me out of my downward spiral.

I shrugged, clearing my throat from the ball of tears trying to break free. "Some internships I want to apply for. Working at the hotel made me realize a direction to go in."

"Finally," Oaklyn muttered.

I rolled my eyes, and she maturely stuck her tongue out at me. Callum shook his head at our antics, snatching the roll from Oaklyn's raised hand and placing it on his plate before she could lob it at me.

"Let me know if I can help. I may have some contacts you might enjoy working with."

"Thanks, I appreciate it." I still had to turn in my application to Carina. I passed by it sitting on the counter every morning, and I ignored it. Not ready to face anything new. I'd been in full wallowing mode. Maybe I'd head home and fill it out tonight. I needed to take steps forward and stop standing still.

All conversation came to a halt when my phone dinged with an incoming message. It clearly said Kent, and Oaklyn's eyes snapped to mine.

My phone dinged two more times, each one sending a flood of adrenaline through my veins. My heart pounded like a racehorse.

Kent: I'm flying in tonight.
Kent: Please let me see you.
Kent: Room 1469. 7pm.

"You shouldn't go, Olivia. Nothing has changed, and you're just hurting you both more," Oaklyn said.

I knew that, but a week away had me forgetting it all, desperate for one more look, and I hated her for pointing out the truth.

Callum's chair scooted back, screaming through the silent room flooding with tension. "I'll take these to the sink." He gathered a handful of plates and bolted, leaving Oaklyn, me, and this decision alone in a standoff.

"Olivia." She tried to get my attention, but I couldn't pull my eyes away from his messages.

Kent. Kent. Kent.

My heart beat in unison with his name, begging me to get up and run to him.

Tears stung my eyes because I knew I'd be letting her down. "I know I shouldn't, but I can't *not* go. I love him."

"Olivia," she said again, harder, pulling my eyes to hers. "Don't do this to yourselves."

I knew I shouldn't. I knew it. But it didn't stop me from standing up and giving in.

"I'm sorry. Tell Cal, thanks for dinner."

Her eyes slid closed but not before I saw the disappointment there.

They were the same feelings I had rushing over me too, but I shoved them down because I needed to see him.

Even if it was the last time, and we only said goodbye.

28 KENT

SHE HAD TO COME. She *had* to.

The minutes ticked by, and my belief that she'd show dwindled.

Maybe I was a fool to ask her to come—a fool setting myself up for more hurt. But I could hurt in her arms for a little while, at least. I could wrap her up and keep her mouth busy to fight off the truth. We could pretend, I just needed her to come.

Thirty-two minutes past the time I told her I'd be here, and still nothing. No messages. No beautiful, vibrant Olivia running through the door. Nothing but silence and the hard thump of my heart.

Then, the click of the door.

As if I held an electrical wire, my whole body zinged back to life. Watching her walk through the door, her mass of golden hair piled on top of her head, her eyes tired but smiling, flooded me with euphoria. I was lighter than I'd been since we'd last seen each other. I had to grip the back of the chair to make sure I didn't float away.

We stared at each other across the small expanse of the room like we hadn't seen each other in years.

Five seconds.

Ten seconds.

Twenty seconds.

I held my breath and counted, needing her to come to me.

Thirty seconds.

Then she was in my arms. A blur of motion colliding with me, locking in the other half to me I'd been searching years for. Burying my nose in her neck, I smelled her warm vanilla scent that mixed with the spice that was all her.

"I missed you," she said against my skin.

"I missed you too."

Missed didn't begin to cover what I'd felt since we'd been apart. Craved, desired, yearned, needed. Nothing began to touch the heavy feeling that'd weighed me down.

But I hadn't known what to do. Nothing had changed between us. She was still afraid of losing Daniel—and I was still unable to keep lying to my best friend, missing her more and more each day.

I hadn't even known I was missing someone so vital in my life until she came and went. Now being without her, I was a half-empty shell.

I'd given her space, hoping she'd come to me. I was unaccustomed to chasing women and hadn't really known where to start, so I did nothing.

In that time, I'd glued myself to Daniel when I could. Hoping he would fill the void—hoping the time I spent with him reminded me why I decided almost twenty years ago to never lie to him again—to never lie about who I was and what I wanted.

"What am I doing here, Kent?" she asked my chest. She'd yet to unwrap her arms from around me, and frankly, she could stay there forever for all I cared.

"I wanted to take you on a date."

Her head tipped back, and damp blue eyes lifted to mine. A slow smile stretched her full lips, making me want to nibble at the lush bottom curve.

I returned her smile and gestured to the candle-lit table with roses and silver domes sitting in the corner. "It's our spot."

And just like that, the smile turned sad, our reality crashing in around us. The reality that we were nothing outside of this room. She swallowed a few times and dashed away the stray tear that broke free before pulling her shoulders back and lifting her regal chin.

No matter how much of a brave face she put on, nothing hid the crack in her soft proclamation. "I can't do this to you. I love you, Kent." Another tear fell, and she didn't bother to wipe it away. "I want you. You know I do, but I can't tell him. He's all I've had for so long, and I don't know who I am without him believing in me."

"He will still believe in you, Olivia. You're not the sum of your body. You are so much more, and just because you're with me, doesn't change that. Why can't you believe that and just tell him?"

"I—I just need more time." The words were hollow, said too many times without any results.

"No, you don't."

We both knew the truth. If she couldn't tell him by now, she never would. Olivia needed to believe in herself. I had to accept that I couldn't do that for her. Maybe some day in the future, she'd reach that point and come back to me. God knows I'd probably still be there waiting.

The pain flooded me to the point of drowning. I couldn't breathe and didn't know what to do. So, I did the only thing I knew how—the thing we were so good at. My words weren't enough, but I'd always been better about expressing my emotions with my body. Even if it was goodbye.

Pulling her into my arms, I wasted no time pressing my mouth to hers. She lifted on her toes and met me halfway. We collided like a supernova. Our feelings coming together in a final explosion before dying out.

"Make love to me, Kent. One more time. Please."

Everything turned frantic, and as much as I wanted to slow down and savor each final touch, I just needed to be inside her.

Without any finesse, I fumbled under her skirt, finding the flimsy lace panties she loved so much and tore them. Her fingers dug into my hair, holding me in place so she could fuse her mouth to mine.

My hands roamed her body, not knowing where to go first. I squeezed her bare ass, hoisting her up enough to move us both to the couch. She leaned back against the arm, her chest thrust out, and I tore down the thin strap of her bra and dress, kissing, licking, and biting my way to her hard nipple.

Taking time to make sure she was ready, I swirled my fingers around her clit, spreading her wetness. I knew when I freed my cock, I'd be a savage—ruthless in getting inside her body.

Playing with her pussy, I kissed up her neck to her ear. "I love you, Olivia."

Her breath hitched, and a restrained whimper broke free, lashing at my heart. "I love you too, Kent." She tugged my hair to press our foreheads together, panting when I pushed my fingers inside.

A pained groan worked its way up my chest, and I flipped her around, needing an outlet for everything inside me. I ripped my pants open and bent my knees, shoving inside. We both cried out from pleasure and pain. I took only a moment to bury my head against the back of her neck and memorize the feel of her wet cunt around me. When she wriggled her hips, trying to move me, I obliged—rutting against her like a wild animal.

One hand latched on to her breast, pinching her nipple. The other was being guided to her throat. Olivia held it there where I could feel every cry of pleasure vibrating her soft neck. Where I could feel the thin chain of my possession still clasped tight. I squeezed softly, wanting to imprint the necklace on her skin, so even if she took it off, it'd always be there.

"Please, Kent," Olivia cried.

Tears splashed against my arm, and fire burned behind my eyes. I couldn't tell you the last time I cried, but having strong, brave, bold Olivia break in my arms, gutted me.

"Please, don't end this."

"I'm sorry, baby. I'm so sorry."

Through it all, I never stopped thrusting. If anything, I fucked her harder, our skin slapping together, mixing with our pain to make the most sorrowful song that would haunt me long after she left.

"Please, don't."

She kept muttering it over and over. *Please, don't stop. Please, don't leave me. Please, don't do this. Please, don't.*

Each one hitting me harder than the last.

I squeezed her throat harder, wanting to give her the biggest high, the strongest orgasm, so it would be impossible to forget.

We were both so consumed by the storm engulfing us, neither of us heard the click of the door opening.

"Vivian said you'd be—"

As if in slow motion, I turned to watch a wide-eyed Daniel, his face morphing from shock to pure, unfiltered rage. The seconds stretched, and I took in the scene from his perspective. My hand around his niece's throat. Her crying. Me buried so deep inside her, I didn't know where I stopped, and she began.

The seconds lasted forever, letting me take in every emotion rolling across his face and feeling the guilt of my actions, seeing the ramifications before they even happened.

"What the fuck?" Daniel roared.

For every second that lasted forever, they moved at warp speed now.

Olivia's muttered, "Oh, my god." Me turning away to cover her. Daniel dropping his cup right before he built speed like a battering ram. I'd barely tucked my cock back in my pants and moved Olivia to the side before he collided, taking us both to the ground.

I vaguely heard a scream, but it was blurred with the way my head smacked the ground, and Daniel climbed on top of me. This —This was why I never wanted him to find out outside of my control.

I did the best I could to protect any vital organs, but not fighting back.

"How could you?" Daniel roared inches from my face. "How could you rape her—*my fucking niece.*"

As if I was expecting a bucket of hot water and was instead doused with ice, my body jerked in surprise. "What? No."

The words didn't even register to Daniel before his fist landed hard on my cheek. Fuck, that hurt.

He gripped my shirt and lifted me up before slamming me back down. Then another slam. "I fucking trusted you."

"I didn't." I tried to say the words, but things were getting fuzzy after so many blows. "Daniel, I didn't."

"Shut up! I saw you. I called you my brother, and I fucking *saw you.*"

"I didn't—"

Another hit and then one more. I was sure I was about to blackout when Olivia's screams finally registered.

"Stop! Just stop. Please, Uncle Daniel. I love him."

The room fell to a hushed silence, and Daniel looked over his shoulder, his fist still raised, and the other clenched tight to my shirt.

"What?"

"I love him. I love him," Olivia said again and again through her tears. Her mascara smeared down her cheeks, and she clutched her dress to her chest, holding up where I tore the strap.

"What he's done to you, Olivia..." He stopped as if he couldn't get the words out. "I don't know what he said to y—"

"He didn't say anything. He didn't *make* me do anything I didn't want to."

Daniel's fist dropped, but he still rested all his weight on my stomach, making it hard to breathe. "But you were crying? He-he—"

"I was crying because we aren't together anymore. I'm losing him, and I love him."

My chest ached with each sob that broke free from the beautiful woman who deserved better than this. I went to push up on my elbows to try and go to her when Daniel used both hands to jerk me up close to his face.

"What did you do to her?"

"Daniel, I—" I tried to defend myself.

"You don't even believe in love, and you let it get this far? What the fuck is wrong with you? She's twenty-one-years-old, of course, she'd think she's in love with you. How could you take advantage of her?"

"He didn't do anything. *I* did. *I* did it all. *I* chased him even when he didn't. It was all *me*."

Daniel slowly lowered me to the floor, the look on his face morphing to confusion and disbelief like he couldn't mesh the Olivia he'd placed on a pedestal and the one admitting she'd chased an older man.

The way she was laying it all out there like she forced herself on me.

I watched his face shift, and I wanted to yank him back to stare at me because as soon as he looked at her, I knew what she'd think. She'd see that look, and every fear would lock into place in her mind.

Regret slammed into me that it got to this point. I knew it was her biggest fear, and I knew, for her, it was about to come true. I needed to get his attention, hit him, and bring it back to me.

But Daniel used my body to adjust himself to face her, and it was too late. Her shoulders dropped, and her arms curled around herself. It was like watching a blossoming flower wilt within seconds.

"Olivia...why?" he breathed.

"Because I'm stupid."

"You're not—" I tried to interrupt.

"Because I wanted him, and I didn't want to be denied. Because he made me happy and excited, and I love him."

Daniel's jaw dropped as he fell to the side, thankfully, off my chest giving me room to breathe.

"Because I'm just some stupid girl."

And with that, she ran. I tried to get up, but my ribs screamed in protest. By the time I was sitting, Daniel was still leaning against the couch, wide-eyed and dumbfounded.

"What the fuck, man?" Slowly, his head turned to me. "You're fucking my niece?"

I winced. When he put it like that, it sounded bad.

"I love her, Daniel."

"So, you—you weren't..."

"God, no. I can't believe you'd think that." I said with a little anger of my own.

He dragged his hands through his hair, tugging on the ends. "Fuck."

"Listen, man, you need to go to her. The reason we were breaking up was because I wanted to tell you, and she was too scared you'd hate her. She needs you more than me. I need you to go to her."

"She what?"

It was good to see he thought it was just as crazy as I knew it was.

"Go. We can talk later."

"You okay," he asked once he was back on his feet.

"Please," I scoffed. "You don't hit that hard."

He rolled his eyes. Before he could walk out, he turned back and leveled me with a serious stare. "I'm going to take care of my niece, but when I'm done, we need to talk. You don't get to just sleep with her without answering a fuck-ton of questions."

"I know."

With a nod, he was gone. I never doubted talking with Daniel would have its issues. I just knew we'd make it through it because we were both open to conversation. I hoped Olivia opened herself to hearing him too before she shut herself off completely.

Groaning, I fell back on the floor, my mind swirling from the abuse and the hope that maybe now that Daniel knew, Olivia would change her mind. That maybe somewhere there was a place for us to work it out.

Or maybe she'd take the out and move on with her future without me. Maybe it wasn't just Daniel that weighed her down, but a future with me.

Jacob's words flooded back, fueling the doubts that maybe once she talked to Daniel, she'd figure out she didn't want me anymore. Maybe she'd only wanted the forbidden, and now that it was gone, so was the love.

Maybe, maybe, maybe.

Too many to keep track of.

Especially with the world spinning as hard as it was.

29 KENT

"Hit me again."

Jackson cocked his brow and looked down at my empty shot glass. "You sure?"

"Do I not look sure?"

"You look drunk."

That was putting it nicely.

"Not drunk enough."

I'd spent the better part of two days blowing off meetings and hoping to drink enough to ignore the fact that I couldn't get Olivia to answer any phone calls, and Daniel had ghosted me. I expected Olivia's avoidance. I expected to have to work on her.

I had *not* expected to not be able to get a hold of Daniel. Had something happened that I'd missed? Had he decided I was some perv that was preying on his niece. If he did, then he could have the decency to say it in person, so I could laugh in his face at how ridiculous that was.

Maybe I'd played this all wrong. Maybe Olivia was right, and Daniel hadn't understood.

Maybe I'd drunk too much because even the thought of

Daniel abandoning me without a word over loving Olivia, was ludicrous. He'd at least go out with a bang.

"You want to talk about it?" Jackson asked, leaning his elbows on the bar.

Voy was mostly empty. Not many people stayed past lunch to get shit-faced.

I tossed the shot back, and maybe that was the reason I muttered my next words so easily.

"I fucked Olivia—a lot. And I love her. *And* I think I fucked it all up."

"Uhhh..." Jackson's eyes widened almost comically. "Daniel's niece?"

I gave him a wink and the gun. "One in the same."

He stood and whistled, pouring another shot. "Damn, Kent."

"Aaaaaaaand, he walked in on us. That's how he found out."

"Fuck me," he muttered, taking my shot and downing it, pouring another for me.

"Yup."

"I take it D didn't take it well?"

"Nope." I squinted, recalling him leaving on, not horrible terms. "Well, I'm not sure."

"What did Olivia do?"

"Bolted."

"You go after her."

"Daniel did."

"But you didn't?" He looked at me like I told him I kicked puppies. Which now that I was saying it out loud, maybe was just as bad as not chasing after her to be by her side.

"She needed Daniel more than me in that moment. As much as I wanted to hold her close to me as tight as I could, she didn't need reassurance from me right then."

"You love her."

"More than anything."

"Does she love you?"

I rubbed my thumb up and down the shot glass, terrified of that answer. "She did." Maybe she got away from Daniel before he could talk to her, and she was alone, blaming me for it all. "I wanted to tell him, and she didn't."

"Why?"

"I don't think enough people tell Olivia how brilliant she is, but Daniel always did, and she was scared to lose that if he found out, we were together."

"That doesn't make sense. He's Daniel. The most understanding guy I know."

"*We* know that." I huffed a laugh. "Olivia is mature in too many ways to count. Hell, she's more mature than all of us combined most of the time. It makes it easy to forget she's still just a twenty-one-year-old girl without all the experience to get her through this."

"So, what does Daniel say?"

"Wish I fucking knew. He hasn't returned any of my calls and took yesterday off from Voyeur."

"*He*," came from behind me, "needed time to process that his manwhore best friend was in love with his niece, who he thinks of as a daughter." Daniel pulled out the stool next to mine and plopped down. "*He* needed time to wipe the sight of you two together from his eyes."

I sipped from my glass, taking the time to process his tone. Not angry, but not playful. We both had things to be angry about. We both had things to apologize for too.

"I know you're old, but there's this thing called text messaging nowadays. All the young kids are doing it."

Daniel rolled his head to the side with a deadpanned glare. "You're a fucking jokester."

"You know how I get when I drink."

"Well, let me get on your level. Jackson, pass that bottle

this way."

Jackson sat the bottle and a glass in front of Daniel. He also placed two waters with a cocked brow. "No fighting. I just cleaned."

And then it was just the two of us. We both stared forward, sipping from our glasses, neither of us speaking. The silence wasn't terrible. Daniel and I had sat in enough silences, it did most of the arguing for us. There was no need to talk.

"I'm sorry I didn't get back to you," he finally said. He poured another shot and tossed it back, filling his glass again before turning to face me. I turned my head and met his serious stare. "I'm sorry I thought the worst. That was a bullshit thing to do because I know you better than I know myself and know that is the last thing that would ever happen. I was shocked, and my brain shut down. I'm the most sorry about that."

"I know." I didn't want to drag it out. Yes, it hurt my feelings and was a heavy blow to handle, but it's not like I'm the definition of level-headed either. We've both had our moments. "I understand. Doesn't mean it didn't suck hearing all that shit, but I get it."

He slapped his hand on my shoulder and went back to facing forward. "How's your head? Obviously, I held back on your face because you're barely bruised."

"Nice lump back there, and you might have cracked a rib. I guess I'm thankful you're too weak to hurt my face."

"Fuck you," he laughed.

Another silence. Another drink.

It was my turn.

"I'm not going to apologize for being with Olivia because I've never been happier than when I'm with her. But I am sorry for how you found out. I should have told you."

"But you didn't, for her."

"I love her." I couldn't meet his eyes when I said it. What if he didn't believe me? What if he thought this was another fling for me and was only there to warn me off his niece? I couldn't take seeing it on his face, so instead, I kept my eyes glued to my glass.

"I know you do."

That had me jerking his way, but he was staring into his own glass.

"I've seen you changing these past few months, calming down a little from your usually rowdy ways. I've seen you wanting to settle down in one spot."

"You have a problem with how rowdy I've been all our lives?"

"Hell, no, but I have to admit, we're getting old, and I'm getting a little tired. And I don't hate the idea of you being here more than you're not."

Laughing, I shook my head. "I never thought I'd see the day where you wanted to settle down."

"Listen," he said, cocking a brow. "I didn't say anything about settling down. I still want to enjoy the variety the world has to offer. I just wouldn't mind doing it at a slower pace."

I tapped my glass to his, then switched out the bottle for the glass of water.

"Did you talk to her?"

I knew the answer from his heavy sigh before he spoke. "She got away too quick, and she's nowhere to be found. Actually, I know where she is, but Oaklyn has threatened bodily harm if I showed up at their house."

"Do you know if she's okay, at least?"

"Oaklyn assured me she's taking care of her. I let her know she had a couple more days before I would happily fight her to get to Olivia."

"Let me know when you do that because I'd love to watch you get your ass kicked by a little girl."

He glared but laughed a little too.

"What are you going to do? We can't leave her this way. She needs you."

"I know." He worked his jaw back and forth. "Family dinner is this weekend, and I'm working with Oaklyn to make sure Olivia is there. She can't avoid me forever."

"Good. Will you—" the lump that had been buried in my throat the past few days tried to make its way back up, choking off my words. "Will you let me know she's okay?"

He nodded, rolling his lips between his teeth. "Was I the only thing standing between you two being together?"

"I think it was the main reason Olivia held back, but I think deep down she was scared to give in completely. I know she's been hurt once, and she didn't want to put herself out there again." I gave Daniel a side-eye. "Must run in the family."

"She may not be my daughter, but she's more like me than she is David. I have to admit, it's a little scary." He ran a hand over his face. "If I send her your way, you'll take care of her?"

"You know, I will."

"There are rules."

"Oh, yeah?" I asked, laughing.

"No PDA in front of me. I don't want to know about any of it."

"Tell her that," I muttered, and he glared. "Okay, okay. I'll make it happen."

"And don't ever bring her to Voyeur. At least not while I'm there and again, I never want to know about it. I give you full permission to lie to me."

He stretched his fist out, and I hit mine against it. "Done."

"Good. Now, have another drink and wish me luck. Olivia is like me in how stubborn she can be, and I'm going to need every ounce of luck I can get to get through to her."

30 OLIVIA

"YOU'RE GOING to your family dinner tonight," Oaklyn proclaimed.

"No."

"Yes. Callum and I haven't had sex since you got here. Desperate times call for desperate measures, and we almost got caught in his office before we could finish. I love you, but I need you gone."

"What if Daniel and Kent are there?"

I hadn't seen either since that day in the hotel. God, what a mess it had been. I'd replayed every nightmare-ish moment over and over. I was haunted by the look on Daniel's face when he realized it was all my fault. That I'd seduced Kent. The moment he realized everyone was right and Olivia Witt was good at being pretty and using her body to get what she wanted.

I shuddered at the thought of having to see that face again.

"Then you act like the mature adult I know you can be, and you face them. I've held your hand and let you mope, doing my best to support you, but it's time for tough love."

"Oh, shit."

"Oh, shit is right, Olivia. You're better than this. You're *stronger* than this. You're smarter than this. You know Daniel loves you and thinks the world of you. You know he would never think less of you. The only person who thinks less of you is you. So, be honest with yourself. If you want to feel sorry for yourself, feel sorry for yourself about the right thing."

"And what's that, miss know-it-all?" God, I was snotty.

"You're scared."

"Of course, I'm scared. I don't want to lose Daniel."

I'd already lost Kent. He'd made it clear more than once that he always chose his best friend over any woman, and I'd been a bitch and pushed him too far. Hell, watching Daniel attack Kent, I may have been the catalyst to end their friendship. All because I wanted to sleep with Kent.

Of course, I was scared. All the outcomes of that night, I could imagine, never ended well, and I wasn't ready to face the consequences.

Oaklyn rolled her eyes, looking like she wanted to bang her head on a wall. "You're scared of being hurt by Kent."

"I'm already hurting because of Kent."

"Yes, but you're controlling it. If you give in—really give in— that opens up a world of possibilities outside of your control. Possibilities that could leave you hurting more than you are now." She gave me a sad smile. "And you're scared."

I tried to scoff, but she wasn't wrong. Leave it up to Oaklyn to shine a light on my darkest corners.

I really was scared of losing Daniel's support. Who would I be without it? It was why I hadn't wanted to tell Daniel about Kent and me. I didn't want to give him an opportunity to look at me differently.

But with Oaklyn's overly bright flashlight glaring down at me, I had to face the other fear. If Daniel gave us his blessing, I'd have nothing stopping me from going all-in with Kent. Nothing from stopping me from falling headfirst and being consumed by the amount of love I have for him. And what if I lost that. I'd been changed and hurt by Aaron, and he was nothing. What would happen if I loved Kent without hesitation and lost it? What would happen to me, then?

That fear was the bigger shadow lurking behind all the others.

"You're a bitch," I said without any heat.

"A bitch that loves you and wants you to be happy. Sometimes that happy comes with a crap-ton of holding our breath and hoping it works out. If you think I'm not doing the same thing with Callum, you're delusional."

"Callum loves you. He'd never hurt you."

"No, he wouldn't. But sometimes life happens, and we have to embrace it. Stop hiding, Olivia. Put yourself out there and grab it. Be the bold bitch I know you can be and take it."

I crossed my arms and sank back into the couch, doing my best to pout. But it was hard to pout when your friend was right. "I hate you."

She plopped down next to me and squeezed me too tight. "I love you too. Now get out because I'm going to be naked when Callum gets home."

"Hot." I waggled my brows. "Need a third? You did work at Voyeur. Maybe I could watch."

She scrunched her nose. "Ew."

For the first time all week, I laughed. Maybe going to dinner and facing this once and for all would be better than hiding. Because the first step in being the fearless Olivia Witt I wanted to be, was to face your fears. And that's what I planned on doing.

THAT BRAVERY LASTED all of an hour to get ready and head to the house.

Now, I stood on the front step, wondering if maybe running away would be better. I wasn't sure how long I stood there, pacing, practicing what I would say for every scenario, but eventually, the door swung open and I froze.

"Okay, I tried to let you come in at your own time, but you've been out here for almost ten minutes now," Daniel said.

I barely held his gaze for the sentence to be over before dropping them to my feet, clasping my sweaty palms together.

"Olivia."

I didn't want to look up, but I didn't want to be this person. I didn't want to be this scared little girl. I wanted to be the woman he expected me to be. So, slowly, I lifted my chin and met his eyes.

He smiled softly. "Hey, kiddo." With a nod, he stepped back, waiting for me to go in.

The house was eerily quiet. Where was Mom greeting me at the foyer? Where was the sound of ice rattling in a glass?

"Where's Mom and Dad? Am I late?'

"On a date."

I whipped around. "What?"

He stood there with his hands in his pockets, rocking back on his heels. "Just you and me tonight."

"Oh."

"Don't look so happy. You used to love when it was just you and me."

"That was before."

"Before what?"

God, why did he have to make me say it? "Before the hotel." I dropped my eyes to the black and white tiles, rolling my lips between my teeth. "Before you saw me the way everyone else does."

His steps clipped across the floor until the tips came into view. He used a finger to lift my chin, making me look at him again. "Olivia, I've always seen what everyone else does."

My heart dropped to the floor, and I wasn't sure how I was still standing. The words vibrated through me, rattling the loosely held armor, shattering it to nothing.

"I see it because that's what you show everyone. But I also see so much more. I see the real you. The determined you. The scared but fierce you."

Tears burned the backs of my eyes, and I bit my trembling lip. "Really?"

"It's easier to show the world what they want to see, but it doesn't change who we really are. And there will be people who come and go and never see past the veneer you wear. There will be people who try to see deeper but are easily convinced there is nothing but the shell." He dipped his head to make sure I could meet his eyes. "Then there are people like me who *know* who you are, inside and out, and there is nothing that would ever change that. No mistake, no atrocity, nothing. You may not be my daughter, but I love you like one."

I couldn't help it, the tears broke free and slipped down my cheeks. "I love you too, Uncle Daniel."

Without hesitation, he wrapped me in his arms, and I buried my head in his chest, feeling a true confidence I wasn't sure I'd ever had slide into place before.

"I'm sorry," I whispered.

"Stop." He gripped my shoulders and held me back so he could see my face. "There's nothing to apologize for."

"I messed up."

His head fell back, and he laughed. "I'm not going to tell you how much I messed up at twenty-one. You're a hell of a lot more mature than I ever was at your age—maybe even now—but no matter how mature you are, you've got a lot of life to screw up.

And you will. It's what you do about them that makes the difference."

"What do I do?"

"What do you want to do?"

I wiped at my cheeks. "Ugh. Can't you just tell me."

Another laugh. "Nope. If you're going to be with my best friend—" he stopped to shudder. "Then I won't be the guide book. You need to figure that man out on your own."

"So, you're not mad I was with Kent?"

He looked around the room and took a deep breath. "It's an adjustment. And I may need therapy, but I've already talked to him and laid out my rules."

"Really? How is he? Is he okay? Are you guys, okay? God, I messed up your friendship. I'm so sorry."

"Stop," he said again. "Kent and I will probably survive the apocalypse together. You didn't mess anything up. As for how he's doing, you need to figure that out on your own."

I paced away from him, rubbing at my forehead. "I messed up so bad. I asked him to hide it even when he explained how much he hated it. Even after he told me about his ex-wife and her asking him to hide himself, I still did it. I was horrible."

"We all make mistakes."

"But what if he can't forgive me. What if he doesn't trust me to be happy with him for him."

"You need to ask him that."

"I don't even know where to start."

He winked. "I have an idea."

31 OLIVIA

"ARE YOU SURE?" Oaklyn asked by my side.

Was I sure about attending Kent's birthday bash? No.

But after my conversation with Daniel last week, I knew what I needed to do. A million things could go wrong. I could put myself out there with this crazy plan I'd concocted, and he could tell me it was too late. The me from months ago urged me to say fuck it and not bother anymore. His loss. But that shell of apathy cracked long ago under the care and ministrations—the love—from Kent. All that was left was an honest need to be with him despite how horrible it could go wrong. Despite that, I had very little control over the outcome. I could get hurt worse than I was already aching. I could break.

Despite all that fear, I knew it was worth it. I had to try. I had to put myself in his hands and hope he didn't let me shatter.

And if everything failed, I had Oaklyn by my side, so if I began to crumble, she could hold me together long enough to get the hell out of there.

"Just hold my hand tonight and support me."

She held out her hand, and I latched on, grateful for the

support. "I've been here the whole time. You deserve this. Be Olivia Witt and take it."

"Sir, yes, sir."

She rolled her eyes and tugged us from the spot we'd been standing on the sidewalk staring up at the hotel I'd had some of my happiest moments in.

The lobby had soft lighting and people lingering with champagne glasses, some even swaying to the jazz playing in the background. I tried not to frantically look from side to side, searching for dark hair sprinkled with flecks of gray.

I was distracted from my search when Vivian greeted us just inside the restaurant where the party was in full swing.

"You made it." She squeezed my hands and pulled me down for a quick hug.

"I wouldn't miss another chance to come back and see you guys."

"We definitely miss you." She craned her neck, scanning the crowd before rolling her eyes and coming back to me. "Alexander is, of course, late. Something about a business call. He can't even stop working long enough to celebrate another year." She smiled and squeezed my hands one more time. "Well, girls, grab some champagne and enjoy the party. I need to go mingle and make sure the VIPs are taken care of."

"Wait," I called before she could go. "I—" I stuttered, but Oaklyn squeezed my hand and reminded me why I was there. "I was wondering if I could ask you a quick favor."

"Of course. Anything," she assured, smiling. I hope that smile stayed in place and didn't transform to one of disgust.

"Okay, I guess I should probably start by explaining." Her head tipped to the side, waiting for me to continue. Taking a deep breath, I word vomited everything on a single exhale. "I love Kent, and we were together before I screwed everything up, and now, I'm trying to get him back because I love him, and I need your help. Please," I added for good measure. Maybe good manners would distract her from me admitting I loved her boss who'd kind of been my boss.

Her brows rising slowly was the only movement she made. "Alexander?"

I winced, biting my lip, and nodded.

"Okay," she said slowly. She shook her head and laughed softly. "Okay," she repeated, this time more firmly. "What do you need me to do?"

"Really? You don't think less of me because I'm in love with the guy I was interning with who's much older?"

Oaklyn scoffed, sick and tired of my doubts.

Vivian smiled softly, and I was sure it was the same look she'd used on her kids when she wanted to reassure them. "Olivia, you're a grown woman. You can make your own decisions, and as long as you respect yourself in the process, who am I to judge how you make yourself happy."

"Oh." She made it sound so simple.

"Like I told my daughter, be with whoever you want or with, however many people you want. Just do it with respect, safety, and pride. And legal. That one's important too," she added, making me and Oaklyn laugh. "Now I know why Alexander has been so damn grumpy all week. So, tell me what you need so we can fix that."

I leaned in conspiringly and laid out my plan. With a few nods, she promised she'd have everything set up for me and left to make it happen.

We'd just turned away when Daniel walked up. "Oaklyn."

"Hey, Daniel."

"Kiddo," he greeted me, reaching his hand out.

I leaned back before he could make contact. "Don't you dare ruffle my hair. It took hours to pin it in place."

He chuckled and held his hands up in surrender. "Wouldn't dream of it."

"Have you seen Kent?"

"Not yet. He said something about a phone call and told me to get started without him."

"Oh."

He squeezed my hand. "Don't worry. He'll be here."

"Okay."

"It's going to be okay, Olivia."

I nodded, but without confidence.

"I need to mingle, but grab yourself some champagne and stop worrying. If you need me, I'm here."

"Thank you, Uncle Daniel."

"I'm always here. Always."

With that reassurance and a kiss to the forehead, he disappeared into the crowd of people, leaving Oaklyn and me alone to wait.

And wait we did.

We found a spot against a wall at the edge of the room and drank glass after glass of champagne, stealing a fresh one every time a waiter stopped by. My mother would be disappointed in my lack of social graces tonight, but my nerves prevented me from being on for strangers. There was only one person I wanted to be on for, and he had yet to arrive.

As the minutes ticked by, my heart sank a little lower, the champagne went down a little quicker. Maybe he wasn't coming. All this stress, all this planning, for nothing. Doubt hung on my limbs, making them heavy and hard to hold up. I wanted to sink to the floor and feel sorry for myself. I downed the contents in my glass and was about to do just that when Oaklyn whispered. "There he is."

She nudged my shoulder, nodding to the entrance.

Every nerve ending came to life, making me ultra-sensitive to the rush of adrenaline surging through my veins. It hurt how hard my heart thumped against my chest when I took in his broad shoulders in a black suit and vest, his snowy white shirt unbuttoned at the top. It hurt when my heart beat irregularly and tried to climb out my throat at his mere presence.

My heart thought me a fool and was ready to abandon my body just to get to him. My heart thought my body was stupid for standing still and watching him move through the crowd, looking delicious and not at all depressed. It screamed at me to screw the plan and run to him, fall at his feet, and beg for forgiveness.

He shook hands and smiled, even managing a laugh. The deep rumble reached across the space and pricked at my eyes, causing tears to build until they fell over.

"I haven't slept all week. Meanwhile, he's looking better than ever."

The more I watched through blurry eyes, the more doubt crept in. Maybe he hadn't been missing me at all. Maybe he was relieved to not have some naïve girl holding him back, asking him to be someone he's not.

"Does he?" Oaklyn asked. She tipped her head to the side as if studying him from all angles. "He looks tired. Even from here, his smile looks forced. Which is saying something for a man who almost always smiles."

I tipped my head like hers and watched him turn away from the group he'd been talking to. His full lips immediately dropped to a flat line. He snagged a glass of champagne from the passing tray and downed it in one go. Maybe Oaklyn was right. Maybe he was hurting too.

Maybe I was letting my fear color what was really there.

Pulling my shoulders back, I swiped the tears from my cheeks just as he looked up and over, locking eyes with mine.

Almost forty feet stood between us, but I felt each emotion slam into me as if it was a physical force.

Hurt.

Longing.

Need.

Desire.

Time stretched on—stood still for us to drink each other in. As if a rubber band snapped, he turned to come to me. Just as quickly, he stopped when Vivian called his name.

"Alexander Kent. It's about time you arrived," she said from the stage where the jazz band played.

He winced before turning to face Vivian, lifting his glass in salute. "It's called fashionably late."

The crowd laughed, and I took that as my chance to slip away. As I made my way along the edge of the room, Vivian kept everyone's attention.

"Well, we have a heck of a party planned for the man of the hour."

"Strippers should be here any minute," Daniel called from somewhere in the crowd. Another rumble of laughter as well as some cheers.

Vivian narrowed her eyes at Daniel and smiled before facing Kent again. "To get the night started, I think we should sing Happy Birthday. What does everyone think?"

I was almost to Vivian as the crowd applauded and cheered.

"To do the honors, we have one of our own, Miss Olivia."

My heart thundered, blood pumping the only sound I could hear. My scalp tingled, and the floor swam. I refused to look out to see his reaction, instead keeping my eyes on Vivian, who held the microphone out to me mouthing *breathe.*

I sucked in a huge gulp of air, and the light claps and shouts of encouragement came roaring back.

"Good luck, Marilyn," Vivian joked.

I don't know why I thought this was such a good idea, but I thought he would laugh, and that was the foundation of who we were together. We had fun, and we loved. He'd once told me that I made him come, and I made him laugh, and those were the two most important things to him. Making him come in front of everyone probably wouldn't go over well at a mostly business function, so I decided to go for laughter.

But when I looked up, he wasn't laughing.

The muscles in his jaw clenched. His Adam's apple bobbed over a swallow. His tongue slicked across his lips. His eyes—almost black from where I stood a few feet away—raked over every inch of my body encased in the nude-colored dress, decorated with rhinestones from head to toe.

He set me on fire, and I had to force my feet to stay in place and open my mouth to sing the words when the band started playing.

I used a breathy voice and worked through my nerves to put on a show. Everyone cheered, and some joined in. When I sang the last word, applause erupted like I'd sung to a stadium and not less than a hundred people.

Kent's eyes never left mine. Each word ignited something in him until I was sure he would explode.

Once things quieted down, I lifted the microphone and put myself out there for him to hold or shatter. There was no hiding behind a façade, there was no pretending in front of anyone. It was just him and me.

"Can I have this dance, Mr. Kent?"

I held my breath as an eternity stretched between my question and his slow nod. With shaking hands, I placed the mic back in the stand and forced myself to walk to his outstretched hand rather than run and jump into his arms. The band broke into a jazz rendition of Stronger by Ziggy Alberts. He loved jazz, and I loved it all. This song was a perfect blend of us.

Holding my breath, I placed my palm in his. Electricity fired from my fingertips, up my arm, jolting my heart, and down to my core, locking everything in place along the way. Without any hesitation, he jerked me into his arms, and I willingly slammed into his chest, sliding my hand around his neck, entangling myself with him.

"Hi," I whispered.

I shivered when his other hand slid around my waist and rested on my bare back. His fingers stroked down to where the dress began just above the crack of my ass. When he didn't say anything, I tracked my gaze up his neck, past his lips, until I finally met his eyes. When I did, he smirked. "Hi."

"Happy birthday."

"Thank you for my song."

"Anything for you," I answered honestly, hoping he heard what I really meant.

"Anything?"

I glared. He wasn't letting me out of this easily. He wanted me to lay it all out there—lay all of myself out there, and I didn't blame him. "Anything. I love you, and I'm sorry for holding any part of myself back because I was scared to give up all control. I was scared of getting hurt. But no matter how much I hid, the truth was always there. I'm all yours, every part of me."

"Olivia," he groaned my name, the deep rumble vibrating against my chest, bringing my nipples to life. "I love you too."

"Can you give me another chance?"

"I'd give you anything you wanted because I'm all yours too."

Euphoria spread like a flood, warming me from the inside out. "I missed you so much. I was such a naïve little girl, and I—I missed you."

"You're anything but a naïve little girl. You're a woman who has been hurt. You're a woman with doubts, and that's allowed for any age. You just have to let me help you through it." He leaned down, pressing his lips against the shell of my ear. "I'm pretty smart with all this life experience I have. Trust your elders. It's good for you."

I buried my head in his shoulder and laughed. "I hope you don't plan on playing the 'elder' card for the rest of our lives."

"The rest of our lives, eh?"

"If you'll have me."

"I don't know how I got so lucky to have you, but I'm not letting you go. You may be in your prime while I'm using a walker, but that's too bad. You get this old man through thick and thin."

"Good. Maybe I find walkers kind of hot."

His head fell back on a laugh, and I fought to not lean in and bite the strong chords of his neck.

Kent twirled me out, and the world spun as he tugged me back in.

"Have I told you how gorgeous you look?"

I bit my lip to hold back my smile. "I may have worn this dress to torture you."

The rough pads of his fingers trailed down each ridge of my vertebrae until they rested just above my ass, where my dress dipped dangerously low.

"I want to rip this part," he said against my ear, dragging his finger along the top crease of my bottom over the dress, "in half, and bend you over to fuck you."

I exhaled shakily and pressed my thighs together to ease the ache only he could cause.

"You promised me anything, and I plan to collect. You know how much I love to bury myself in your tight ass."

"Yes," I hissed. "Do it."

A rumble started low in his chest, and his eyes melted with promise. "Take me home, Olivia. Otherwise, I'm going to break one of Daniel's rules and fuck you right here, and he's already glaring enough.

"I can't wait for home, Kent. I need you now."

"How about one last time in our room."

I was already turning to walk out when I answered. "If we make it."

We didn't end up making it. He made good on his promise and ripped my dress down the back and fucked me in the elevator.

It was perfect.

It was us.

EPILOGUE

OLIVIA

"I'm sorry. Who?" my mom asked as my dad choked on his wine.

"I'm seeing Kent."

"Is this a boy from school?"

"No. This is Alexander Kent. Uncle Daniel's friend."

"I'm going to need something stronger," my dad mumbled, downing his full glass. He rubbed a hand down his face, and then stood from the dining room table to go to the liquor cabinet, poured himself a glass, and downed that too.

My mom still sat there staring, her face frozen in a mix of shock and concern.

"I know it's not what you would consider ideal, but I'm happy." My chest expands to near exploding, and I can't stop the full smile stretching my cheeks until they ache. "I'm really happy, Mom."

Her face softened, taking in the joy pouring off me. "I mean... I—" she laughed softly. "I'm not really sure what to say."

"Does Daniel know?" Dad asked.

"Yes." They didn't need to know how he found out.

"Jesus," my dad mumbled again before taking another drink.

"Daddy?" I needed him on board. Or at least willing to climb on board. Daniel and Kent were on their way here for dinner, but I came early because I planned on kissing Kent hello and holding his hand through dinner. I would never hide my love for him again.

"He's so old."

"He's hardly that old, but it doesn't matter. As long as he makes me happy, that should be all you care about."

"You know that's all I want for you," Dad said.

"As long as you're happy, baby girl," Mom added.

Happiness bubbled over, and a giggle broke free. "I really, really am. He pushes me to be better—challenges me. And I like to think I do the same for him."

My dad gave a resigned sigh, but I could see that he was happy that I was happy. It was enough. My mom smiled and squeezed my hand.

The doorbell rang, and we all froze, knowing who was on the other side.

"I'll get it." Before I stepped out, I turned to my parents. "Please don't make it weird."

"Wouldn't dream of it," my dad said dryly.

My mom rolled her eyes. "I promise to keep the awkwardness to a minimum."

"Thanks, Mom."

Opening the door, I only held back from jumping into Kent's arms because Daniel stepped between us with a cocked eyebrow. "Remember. PDA to the bare minimum. Preferable to zero."

Scoffing, I shoved him out of the way and tugged a nervous-looking Kent through the door and into my arms. "Relax," I whispered against his ear.

"I'll relax when your dad doesn't shoot me."

"They're fine. I just got done talking to them. Dad may be drunk by now, but it will be fine. Besides, if Daniel didn't shoot you, my dad surely wouldn't."

"True," Daniel laughed. "Lucky for you, David is a happy drunk."

Another nervous laugh from Kent and then I was tugging him to the dining room. My mom stood and briefly glanced at our joined hands before greeting Kent as she always did with a hug and a kiss to his cheek.

"Alexander, I'm so glad you could make it."

"Thank you for having me."

It all felt more formal, but I figured it would be for a while. It was new and not what anyone expected. At least it wasn't awkward.

Or it wasn't until Dad spoke up.

"You hurt her, and I'll fucking kill you."

"David," my mom gasped.

Daniel choked on his water, not even bothering to hide his laughter.

"Wouldn't dream of it, Sir."

"God, Kent, don't make it weird and call me Sir. I've known you for years."

I nudged Kent with my shoulder. "Yeah, Kent. Way to make it awkward."

He glared softly at me. To everyone else, it was a cute stare, but to me, I saw the promise of what was to come tonight.

And I couldn't wait.

But first, I needed to sit at our family dinner with my boyfriend and enjoy never hiding my love for him again.

A few months later

"Can you not cook anything?"

"Olivia. What about me living out of a hotel and eating at my parents says I'm a hidden culinary artist?" Kent deadpanned.

"It's pasta, Kent," she said like it explained everything. "Pasta."

"It's not, you can do it."

She scoffed and stuttered over her words. "I—I'm still young. I have years to learn how to cook."

She was so sexy when she put on the haughty, snobby, rich girl look. It made me all the more excited to dig underneath it and make her beg for me.

"You know what I'm good at," I asked, tossing the pan of burnt noodles into the sink.

"We don't have time for this," she said, trying to glare, but I saw the spark of need flickering.

I stalked over, loving that she didn't back away. By the time I reached her, her chest was heaving under her silky top. Wrapping my arm around her waist, I tugged her to me hard and leaned down to her ear, stroking my fingers along her thigh. "I do this thing with my fingers..."

"Uh-huh," she breathed when I left her hanging.

"It's called ordering in. I dial the number, and they make me what I want."

She jerked back as far as I'd let her go and glared at me, slapping my chest when she saw me laughing.

"It's our first dinner party together. I didn't want to order in. And you're a tease."

"Says the girl in tight leather pants and some silky top with no bra."

She shoved away from my chest and looked down at her chest like she'd find her shirt see-through. "I don't need a bra."

"It's still a tease." We glared at each other, cocking a brow, waiting for the other to break.

"Ugh," she groaned when she blinked.

"Now, tell me where you want to order from."

"If we order from that Italian place now, it can get here quick, and we can put it in dishes like we made it."

"On it."

Everything arrived with just enough time for us to stuff the aluminum tins into the trash. I'd moved into her apartment two weeks ago. I'd waited until the sale could go through before I officially called this place home. I wasn't going to live with my girlfriend in the apartment her father paid for. Not that it'd stopped me from staying here almost every night since we announced our relationship.

A couple nights ago, we'd been watching the Food Network, and she'd had this grand plan to have everyone over for a dinner party to celebrate. Who was I to deny her? Frankly, it wasn't like I could if I tried.

The doorbell rang, and it was like everyone arrived at once.

"Did you all take a cab together?"

"Not with these two burly men," Carina groaned, gesturing to her baby-daddy, Ian, and Oaklyn's boyfriend, Callum.

"Whatever," Ian scoffed. "Little Miss Audrey takes up all the room with her car seat and awesome personality. Isn't that right, baby?"

"Here we go with the baby talk," Hanna said with a roll of her eyes.

Carina had called earlier and asked if she could bring Hanna along, and of course, Olivia said the more, the merrier. Hanna was Ian's business partner's little sister, and Carina had taken to her after a rough start.

Frankly, I was happy to see her there because she made Daniel squirm. He'd met the girl only a handful of times, and each one he'd been unable to take his eyes off her. She, of course, stuttered and blushed each time he got too close.

It was cute.

"Knock, knock."

Speak of the devil. Daniel stepped through the open door behind everyone else.

"Welcome," Olivia greeted everyone.

"Hey, kiddo." Daniel pulled her in for a hug and kissed the top of her head.

"Dinner is all ready, so let's take a seat."

Daniel raised his fist, and I bumped my knuckles with his. "Daniel, you can sit next to Hanna."

He jerked a glare my way, and I just smirked in return.

This would be fun.

Don't miss a thing and add Teacher, Daniel and Hanna's story, to your Goodreads TBR. Coming in 2020.

See where the Voyeur series all began in the forbidden, student-teacher romance, VOYEUR.

If you're looking for a little more angst in your books you can check out my new adult, second chance romance, SHAME. Find out how Anna and Kevin discover each other and learn to understand their unique sexuality.

Don't miss out on any of my upcoming books, giveaways, and

important news by signing up for my newsletter... Fiona Cole Newsletter.

You can also join my Facebook reader group, Fiona Cole's Lovers, for exclusive sneak peeks and teasers.

ACKNOWLEDGMENTS

My family: Thank you for always understanding and supportive. Thank you for the cuddles after a hard day and laughs when all I want to do is rip my hair out. I couldn't do this without you being the foundation holding me up. I love you.

Karla. Dream Team, baby.

Serena. It's been over a year since you became my PA and I'm thankful each and every day to have you by my side. I would be a sobbing mess in a corner without you.

Najla Qamber. The best damn cover designer there ever was. Thank you for all your talent. Thank you for always hearing my vision and turning into perfection.

Linda. Thank you for holding my hand and petting my hair when I'm on the verge of crawling in a hole. I couldn't do this without you or your enthusiasm. I appreciate everything you do and can't wait to drink wine together some day.

Kelly. Thank you for being an amazing editor. Thank you for being an even better friend! You give me the confidence to publish a book I know is the best it could be because of you.

Michelle and Julia. Thank you for always being able to beta read. You ask the hard questions and offer such amazing suggestions. Thank you for helping me make the story better than I could've imagined.

Review team. You ladies are wonderful, fun, kind, and beyond supportive. Thank you for every share, every review, and everything in between.

Lovers. You guys are my safe place. You guys give me the best book recommendations and make me laugh. You're more than I could ever ask for. I can't tell you how many times I've scrolled through your comments and have been brought to tears. Thank you for being such an awesome group.

Bloggers. To every single one from personal pages to the bookstagrammers. You all work so hard and take beautiful pictures and write such amazingly kind words in reviews. I don't have enough words to let you know how much you all mean to me. I couldn't do this without you.

Readers. You guys rock my socks off. Thank you for taking a chance on my words. Thank you for taking the time to read something I've created. You're the best.

ABOUT THE AUTHOR

Fiona Cole is a military wife and a stay at home mom with degrees in biology and chemistry. As much as she loved science, she decided to postpone her career to stay at home with her two little girls, and immersed herself in the world of books until finally deciding to write her own.

Fiona loves hearing from her readers, so be sure to follow her on social media.

Email: authorfionacole@gmail.com
Newsletter
Reader Group: Fiona Cole's Lovers

www.authorfionacole.com

ALSO BY FIONA COLE

The Me Series

Where You Can Find Me

Deny Me

Imagine Me

Shame Me Not Series

Shame

Make It to the Altar (Shame Me Not 1.5)

The Voyeur Series

Voyeur

Lovers (Cards of Love)

Savior

Another

Liar

Teacher (Coming Spring/Summer 2020)

Made in United States
Orlando, FL
12 September 2022

22320596R10152